TERROR STATION

By
DWIGHT V. SWAIN

I0541451

ARMCHAIR FICTION & MUSIC
PO Box 4369, Medford, Oregon 97504

DESERT OF THE DOOMED

There was something strange going on at the secluded, top-secret military base out in the middle of the southwestern desert. The base's security chief, Carl Stone, had just returned from an important trip to Washington D. C. He noticed it almost immediately—a distinct change in his comrades' perceptions. It was clear that something was horribly wrong. The entire contingent of military personnel appeared to have a tenuous grasp on reality—and what was that constant buzzing sound?

Suddenly there was sheer madness and monstrous creatures appearing out of nowhere. Yet Stone knew it was not madness he was fighting—but a vicious mind-controlling enemy.

The stake: Earth!

FOR A SECOND COMPLETE NOVEL, TURN TO PAGE 95

CAST OF CHARACTERS

CARL STONE
Head of Security for a top-secret military base. Could he break the alien spell in time?

JOHN MACDOUGAL
Being head of the top secret project called, "The Project" was important to him—and he wasn't willing to lose that position.

DR. REVA ADAMS
She was the Base Psychiatrist…Carl's ex. Was she an innocent victim or an alien collaborator?

GLINES
This fat, sweaty man was just a lowly secretary, but maybe he wanted more…

QUINN
What was that faint and highly annoying buzzing sound? And why was he the only base resident who could hear it?

SGT. BJORNBERG
A good soldier just following orders, right? But just whose orders were they?

DAWES
To say he was puzzled by some of his new orders regarding "The Project" was a huge understatement.

CHAPTER ONE

HE saw the woman first. Blindly, she stumbled out of the moonless desert night a hundred yards ahead, into the dim right edge of the path slashed by his headlights. Lurching, staggering, she scuffed through the gravel of the highway's shoulder; reached the asphalt and took two short, uncertain steps out on it, swaying as if the sudden change to smoother footing had almost made her lose her balance.

Stone jammed on his brakes.

Only then, before the car could even start to stop, movement flickered in the murk from which the woman had emerged. Stone glimpsed a shifting scarlet glow, a dipping, twisting streak of color. Oozing through the backdrop of the night, it drew swiftly closer to the roadway and the woman...then faded, swallowed up in the glare of the approaching headlights.

But as it vanished, a spot of strange translucence materialized to replace it.

Formless, almost without perceptible substance, the splotch moved faster now, gliding across the shoulder and out onto the highway.

Beyond it, the woman half-turned; threw a frantic glance back along the way from which she'd come even as she took another stumbling step.

In the same instant, the translucence swept down upon her.

The woman's face contorted. Sheer terror etched her features, so deep that even Stone could see it. She tried to lunge away.

Terror Station

by

Dwight V. Swain

It was sheer madness — monstrous creatures appearing out of nowhere at a top-secret desert Base. Yet Stone knew it was not madness he was fighting but a vicious enemy.   The Stake: Earth!

But now gleaming tendrils lanced forth from the translucence, curled about her, held her helpless.

The woman screamed.

That scream: It echoed even through the shriek of Stone's scorching tires, seared itself into his brain so deep that he never would, never could, forget it.

Then, abruptly, the scream cut off. The translucence swirled back towards the roadside and the shadows, dragging the woman with it.

Savagely, Stone jerked the steering wheel right with all his might, trying to follow the horror with his headlights. Skidding, the car rocked round on two wheels. For a spine-chilling split second Stone thought it was going to go over. But at the last moment it righted itself and shuddered to a halt in a choking cloud of dust beyond the shoulder.

Straight ahead, woman and translucence hung spotlighted less than fifty feet away.

Stone snatched his Colt from its holster on the steering post. Leaping from the car, he raced forward.

It was as if the sight of him gave the woman new strength. Her whole body convulsed. Tearing free from the monstrous thing that held her, she lurched towards Stone, blood streaming from a dozen wounds.

The translucence seemed to swell and darken. Then, in a rush, it hurtled towards the woman.

But now Stone was abreast of her. Cat-footed, he leaped between her and the monster; he blazed three fast shots into its center.

The shining surface quivered. For the fraction of a second it drew back.

Stone could see the creature more clearly now. Murkily transparent as oily water, it stood nearly a head taller than his own six feet.

Except that it didn't have any head.

Instead, a barrel body splayed out into many thin, cable-like tentacles at top and bottom, each terminating in a round disc the size of a quarter. Its only truly opaque matter appeared to be concentrated in a narrow, dully scarlet band perhaps three inches wide that girded the center of its body.

Staring at it, Stone wondered if he were somehow going mad.

Then, abruptly, there was no more time for thinking, observation. With a rush, the monster lunged towards him, moving on its lower tentacles as if they were so many skillfully-coordinated feet.

Behind Stone, the woman cried out: "The light—! Watch out for the light!"

STONE glimpsed it as she spoke: A small, lensed cube of box that suddenly shot out at the end of one of the creature's upper tentacles.

He leaped sidewise.

Almost in the same instant, a vivid purple streak blazed from the box.

It missed Stone by inches. Desperately, he snapped a wild shot at the lens, then fired twice more in the onrushing monster's midriff.

This time, the thing didn't even hesitate.

Stone jerked the trigger again.

A hollow click. The gun was empty.

With a curse, Stone hurled it at the nightmare thing before him. Then, whirling, he raced headlong back towards his car.

Like an evil, gleaming shadow, the monster sped after him. It moved fast—horribly, incredibly fast.

Panting, Stone veered left, not even daring to look back. The headlights blazed blindingly into his eyes.

Something brushed his shoulder. He felt his shirt rip.

Then he was past the lights. Twisting, he dived headlong beneath the car, heedless of the gravel that slashed his face and chest and knees and shins and belly. Driving his elbows into the dirt, he whipped himself out on the far side of the vehicle.

A tentacle groped for his heel.

Savagely, he stamped the disc against a rock.

The tentacle jerked back. Sobbing for breath, Stone scrambled to his knees and clutched the doorhandle.

He got the door open just as another tentacle came through the window on the far side of the car, reaching for him.

Cursing, he jerked back barely in time, slammed the door shut on the tentacle with all his strength.

The latch caught. The car shook as the monster tried to writhe away.

Stone spun about. In three steps he was at the trunk—clawing aside his luggage, breaking his nails on the jack.

His hand closed around the axe handle in the same instant that the car gave a sudden lurch. There was a sound like that of a gigantic rubber band snapping. Then, like an echo, a tentacle-disc slapped against his right ribs just below the armpit.

Clutching the axe, Stone leaped back.

But the disc clung as if it were part of him. Agony exploded around it, tearing at his flesh. Before he could shake the red haze of pain from his eyes, the monster free of the car now—was upon him.

Convulsively, Stone swung the axe.

It bounced off the barrel body as if it had struck solid rubber. More discs slapped at him.

Stone staggered, axe sagging. The tentacles had him now—constricting, engulfing. He lurched against the monster; felt the discs' pressure growing, seeking to rend his very body.

Pain-knotted, barely conscious, he twisted the axe-blade against the opaque scarlet band that girded the creature's midriff.

Reflex-like, a disc low on his spine jerked him back, away.

Stone forgot the agony, the pain-haze. Fiercely, he slashed out with the axe.

A surge of triumph raced through him as its blade bit deep into the unshielded scarlet band.

Now the tentacles tore at him in frenzy, clutched at the axe.

Before they could seize it, Stone swung again—horizontally, this time, so that the rubbery body might have no chance to deflect the cutting edge from the nerve-band.

The blade struck home with a sound like that of a melon shattering on pavement. Clear to the eye it sank—

The tentacles hurled Stone backward, slamming him hard against the side of his car as they let go their hold. He sagged there, raw-nerved and sick and bleeding.

Shambling, uncertain, the monster moved away...away—and towards the spot where the woman still lay prone and silent.

With an effort, Stone dragged himself erect. Then, axe still in hand, he stumbled after the nightmare creature.

The thing speeded its pace.

Stone forced himself to a run, cutting wide around his adversary.

Ten seconds later, he stood between it and the woman.

The creature hesitated.

STONE bared his teeth in a savage grimace. The fact that he had outdistanced the hideous thing; that it paused now, grasping and indecisive—such were more than enough to strip away his own pain and weariness.

"Damn you!" he grated harshly. "We'll see who gets her!"

He lifted the axe; took a quick step forward.

The monster fell back before him.

Then, of a sudden, a tentacle speared out.

—The tentacle with the lightbox.

Stone charged in, swinging, as the purple streak blazed forth.

The creature shifted, undulating away from the axe. The streak of purple fire missed Stone.

Missed, by far too wide a margin to be coincidence.

Like an echo, a choked cry of agony rose behind him.

Stone spun about, numb panic flaring in him.

The woman no longer lay limp and prostrate. Now, instead, her whole body jerked in a continuing spasm. Her hands clutched her side, and her lips spilled blood.

Stone whirled again, back to the monster.

But the creature was already fleeing—gliding out of the arc of the headlights' beam, into the empty blackness of the desert. Even as Stone glimpsed it, the night swallowed it up.

Only a lunatic would have followed.

With a snarl of frustration, Stone ran to the woman; dropped on his knees beside her.

Her whole side was burned black where the purple beam had struck. She clutched his hand, her nails biting deep. "Kill me, quick! Please! I can't stand it—"

Sweat stood out on Stone's forehead. Desperately, he forced his voice gentle, level: "Easy, now. You'll be all right. I'll get you to my car. It's only a couple of miles to the proving ground—"

"No, no. I can't stand it. I'm dying—" The woman's voice trailed off in a bubbling scream. Her body twisted. Then: "Maybe—my husband—the robots—back there beyond the mesa—"

"Easy…" Stone whispered. But his lips were dry.

"My…my husband…"

A shudder ran through the woman's body. Then, suddenly, she sagged limp.

Dead.

Sickness twisted at Stone's belly. Gently, he crossed the woman's arms across her breasts…straightened the tormented twisted body…wiped away the blood and smoothed the dark hair back from the small, plain face.

She was young, he saw now; far younger than he'd thought—not more than twenty-five at most.

So young…and so dead.

And somewhere, out there in the desert night, lurked the creature that had killed her.

And what was it the dying woman had said, about robots on a mesa—?

Stone's spine prickled. Stiffly, he started to get up.

Only then, out of the night, a voice clipped, "Hold it!"

A chill, somehow familiar voice.

Stone froze.

"That's it. And get your hands out where we can see 'em."

Wordless, Stone obeyed.

"Now turn so the light shines on your face."

Again, obedience.

"Well! If it isn't our Mister Stone!" The words carried an ugly inflection. And then: "Come on, you guys…"

Figures converged from the blackness—erect, helmeted, uniformed figures, armed with rifles and carbines.

Soldiers.

The tension drained out of Stone. Of a sudden he felt weak, wobbly, half-hysterical.

And that voice—of course it was familiar!

"Sergeant Bjornberg," he announced, "I've never been so glad to see anybody in my life!"

He dropped his hands.

Instantly, a gun-barrel gouged his back. "Keep those hands out!"

"What—?" Stone stared. "Sergeant, you know me…"

"Do I? Don't try to pull any fast ones on me, mister!" The sergeant moved into view as he spoke. His usually good-humored features showed heavy now, set in sullen lines. Striding over to the woman, he flashed a light onto her dead face. "Well, now! Ain't this pretty!"

With an effort, Stone held his temper. "The way she was killed was anything but pretty, sergeant. And the thing that did the job is still running loose. I'd suggest you post a heavy guard, then get me to headquarters as soon as possible."

The sergeant sneered openly.

"*You're* telling *me* what to do?"

"I'm merely suggesting." In spite of himself, Stone's voice took on a brittle edge. "However, I do happen to have charge of certain aspects of security for this area, and I doubt that Captain Hayes would think I was out of line."

"Oh?" Sergeant Bjornberg grinned—an ugly grin, utterly without mirth. "Well, I think I got a better idea, *Mister* Stone."

"Well?"

"I'll post a guard, all right; and I'll take you to headquarters."

"Fair enough."

"But I'll do it my own way, you lousy civilian phony—and that's under arrest, as a prisoner and a murder suspect!"

CHAPTER TWO

GLINES' taste ran to richly aromatic tobaccos. Even now, long after midnight, his office hung heavy with the stink of the stuff.

Stone wrinkled his nose in distaste, again shifted his weight in the hard chair trying to ease his aching muscles. The welts where the monster's discs had clutched him stung like new burns. Bruises and scratches plagued him every time he moved, a continuing, continuous irritation.

And still Glines did not come.

Now, in the silence, the ticking of the leather-embellished desk clock seemed to grow louder, till the sound of it echoed in Stone's ears like an infuriating off-key drumbeat. He found himself resenting the desk itself, with its precise, too-neat arrangement of office trivia. The air the lazy ceiling fan pushed against his face pressed thick as warm, wet cheesecloth.

Yet his mouth stayed dry. When a rill of icy sweat trickled from his armpit, it sent a tremor through his whole body.

He gritted his teeth, squeezed his eyes tight shut, trying to shut out the awful memory of the monster and the woman.

But shutting his eyes only made the picture come back clearer, sharper. Better to leave them open...

Once more, he shifted cursing under his breath as new pain pulsed through him.

Besides, the chair creaked.

Stone frowned. It was idiotic, the way he found himself giving way to every tiny irritation...almost as if the whole base—this office especially—somehow had come to radiate tension.

And tension was one thing he couldn't afford just now.

Grimly, he sucked in air—a deep breath that filled his lungs...held it for the count of ten...expelled it in a rush, letting himself go limp and jelly-like.

The third time he did it, he knew that some of the raw-nerved stiffness was leaving him. Closing his eyes no longer conjured up macabre visions.

Now, however, he found his mind turning to Bjornberg.

The sergeant's open hostility baffled him. In the past, they'd always been on a pleasant enough footing—friends, almost. Back in his service days, he'd even soldiered in some of the same places as had the sergeant. It gave them a common ground of past and interest, something to talk about over a beer.

Yet tonight, Bjornberg had called him a "lousy civilian phony".

Stone shook his head slowly. It just didn't make sense.

He became aware that the clock's tick was growing louder again...fraying at his nerves—

Then, abruptly, footsteps echoed in the hall outside. The door opened. Glines waddled in.

It was typical that he should be freshly shaven and fully dressed, even to tie and clean white shirt. Emergencies might come and go; but if they wanted Glines' attention, they'd have to wait till the last button was properly secured and the pink chops smooth and anointed with perfumed shaving lotion.

With an effort, Stone kept his voice pleasant. "Hi, Herb. Sorry to drag you out with this nonsense."

"Nonsense—?" Glines' fat face stayed stiff, his manner unbending. "I'm not sure I like your choice of words there, Stone."

Stone stared. "Herb! What is this? Just because you take over my job for two weeks while they call me in to Washington—"

"Don't evade the issue, Stone!" Glines posed, too erect, beside the desk. His lips pursed. "As I see it, neither your job nor your trip to Washington has anything to do with the things Sergeant Bjornberg's told me."

"I see." Stone clipped his words. "In that case, Glines, maybe we'd better get a few things straight. It happens I'm your superior here. And if I'm not 'Carl' to you, then I'm damn well '*Mister* Stone.' Is that clear?"

"No."

"What—?"

"No, I said. It isn't clear—not clear at all." Glines stood openly defiant, insulting. Insolently, he thrust out his puffy lower lip. "You talk a lot about being my superior here, don't you? Well, as of this moment, I'm not at all sure that you are."

Stone drew a deep, incredulous breath. Then, slowly—very slowly—he came up from his chair. When he spoke, his words were measured: "Glines, you're either drunk or crazy. In either case, I'm sick of it. The MP's have my statement of the facts of what happened tonight. I'm worn out, and I want to get a shower and have the medics disinfect these cuts and then go to bed. This cross-examination business can wait till morning."

He turned on his heel, strode towards the door.

Behind him, a drawer rattled. Glines' voice rang, shrill and angry:

"Oh, no, you don't!"

Stone ignored him.

"Stone! Stop or I'll shoot!"

Stone came up short; half-turned, staring.

GLINES stood crouched behind the desk, his eyes black, beady slits above fat cheeks. He gripped an automatic, a heavy Army Colt, in one pudgy hand.

"Back!" he cried shrilly. "Come back here, Stone, before I shoot you like you deserve!"

Stone stood very still, trying without avail to fathom the things that seethed in the black eyes.

First Bjornberg; now Glines. Had the whole base gone mad?

"Easy, Herb," he said soothingly. "Easy does it. I'll come back."

Careful of every movement, he made his way to the desk. "You can put the gun down now, Herb. I won't try to leave again till you say to."

"I'll say you won't!" Glines bared uneven teeth in a taunting smile. And then: "Oh, you were clever, all right, Stone. But not clever enough to fool me."

"I wasn't?"

"No. It all came to me in a flash as soon as Bjornberg told me about you and that woman, and the crazy story you tried to put out about fighting some monster."

Glines' face grew more flushed as he spoke, his words and breathing jerky and uneven. The hand that held the gun quivered.

New prickles of tension touched Stone's spine. "Sure, Herb; sure…"

It was as if his fat little aide hadn't even heard him; as if the man were talking to himself, almost.

"The minute I woke up, it all clicked into place. Just like that." Glines giggled, high and ragged. "Oh, I'd been suspicious all along, of course. I checked your record while you were gone—the way you sneaked into security work, pretending to be an American agent while you fought with the Communists in Spain; the business of playing professional soldier in China; those years you spent with the OSS during the war. You cut quite a figure, all right. It made you look tough, dangerous, trustworthy, experienced. But it was all aimed at just one thing: This job here, in charge of civilian security on the country's top top secret project. You were willing to wait, to bide your time. Because you knew that when you got this spot here you could really do the job right when you betrayed us!"

A numbness crept over Stone. It was incredible, this mad net of distortion Glines was weaving about him.

Something was behind it, surely…some dark and evil pattern.

Yet what—?

It was a question pregnant with frustration. Because he didn't dare to argue; not with an obvious madman. He couldn't even probe too deeply.

He tried to speak calmly: "Did you figure out the rest of it, too, Herb?"

"The rest—?"

"Sure. How it all fits together. How the business about the woman and the monster could help me betray anything?"

Scorn distended Glines' eyes. He radiated contempt. "Do you think I'm completely stupid? I knew it the instant I woke up, of course, just like the rest. You wanted some kind of cover to hide behind so that no one would suspect you when news about the project got out. So you killed that poor woman, then made up the story about the monster. You knew that as soon as it got to the papers there'd be dozen's of reporters swarming over the base; you can't guard every inch of a government reservation as big as this one. Then you could blame the reporters for the leak on the project."

"I see." Stone nodded slowly. "Well, I guess you've got it all, then. You might as well call in MacDougal."

"Don't worry. I'll call him." Again Glines giggled. "Only first I'm going to wrap this all up good and tight. You're too good a friend of his for me to take any chances. Besides,"—his eyes grew suddenly cold and wary—"besides, I'm not too sure where he stands. Even a base director's suspect, when he's friends with a traitor!"

STONE made an elaborate business of shrugging. "That's carrying it a little far, isn't it, Herb? Mac's going to have the final report to make on this business, and he might not like it if he thought you were trying to pull a fast one on him."

"If he knew, he might." Glines' eyes glittered. "But then, I plan to handle it more simply than that, without any red tape. Bjornberg understands. He'll take care of it."

"He'll—take care of it?"

"Yes." Glines smirked. *Ley del fuego*, they call it in Spanish. The law of flight. Shot while attempting to escape."

Stone's palms were suddenly slick with sweat. The ticking of the desk clock echoed in his ears like the knell of doom.

He made it a point to breathe deeply, evenly. "That's a big responsibility for a man to take, Herb."

"Let me worry about that, Stone. I think I'll find it a pleasure."

As he spoke, Glines came round the desk, waddling as always.

Ordinarily, the way Glines moved made Stone want to smile. Only now, of a sudden, it wasn't funny.

Especially when the gun the fat man held stayed so very steady.

Abruptly, ignoring the weapons, Stone turned to the desk...picked up the clock...stared down at its face. "You'd better hurry, then, Herb."

"What—?"

"Time's running out. The sergeant goes off duty in a couple of minutes."

He lifted the clock so Glines could see it.

The black, beady eyes flicked to the dial.

Stone hurled the clock, square at Glines' head.

His aide jerked away, barely in time to dodge the missile.

But in that split second of distraction, reflex movement, Stone lunged in—knocking Glines' gun aside with a left-foreman block, driving a hard right into the pit of the fat man's bulging paunch.

Glines crashed back against the wall, tottered, and slid to the floor his face scarlet as he fought agonizedly for breath.

Stone stomped down on his wrist; kicked the Colt aside. Then, scooping it up, he stood straining his ears, listening for some outside reaction to the scuffle.

None came.

Wordless, he strode to the door. Panting, now, Glines glared up at him eyes sparking hate. "Go—go ahead—Stone! See—how far you get!"

"Bjornberg?"

"That's right. I gave him orders to stand guard outside the building—and to shoot on sight!"

Stone smiled thinly. "That's why I'm not going out." He threw the door's heavy bolt in place. "You see, there's just one catch to all your theories, Glines: They're not true. So we're going to get MacDougal down here right now and square things away."

As he spoke, he strode swiftly to the desk; picked up the phone, dialed the base director's quarters number.

Four rings. Then MacDougal's sleep-thickened voice: "Base director speaking."

"Carl Stone, Mac. Get down to Glines' office fast; this is urgent. And it might be smart to bring along a couple of guards."

The sleepiness faded from MacDougal's voice. "Of course, Carl. If you say so." A pause. "I didn't know you were back. When did you get in?"

"Awhile ago. But something's happened I don't want to talk about on the phone, and I can't leave the office, here."

"I'll be there in five minutes."

HE made it in four—a big, shaggy man with shoulders like mine beams and John L. Lewis eyebrows. Two armed guards followed him in.

"You've got troubles, Carl?"

"You might say so. Glines, here"—Stone gestured to the fat man, still sitting slumped against the wall—"has suddenly decided I'm a traitor. His solution to the problem was to arrange to have me shot while attempting to escape."

MacDougal's shaggy eyebrows lifted. "Well, now! That's one way of eliminating a problem, isn't it? —Though I doubt that he's actually got it in him to pull the trigger when the cards are down."

Stone shrugged. "He didn't plan to."

"No?" The base director cocked his head. "Then tell me just who—?"

"Sergeant Bjornberg. Whether he shares Glines' delusions or not, I can't say. But Glines tells me he stationed the sergeant outside the building, with orders to shoot me on sight."

MacDougal frowned. "Things really have been happening to you, haven't they, Carl?" And then, turning to Glines: "How about this, Herb? Got anything to get off your chest?"

The fat man scrambled to his feet and stood pompously erect in a belated effort to regain his dignity. His eyes sparked. "I certainly do, Mr. MacDougal. There's not a word of truth in what he says—about the shooting part, that is. What actually happened was, Sergeant Bjornberg caught him down the road a couple of miles, crouched over a woman's corpse. You can see how cut up he is"—a contemptuous gesture towards Stone—"as if they'd fought before he killed her. He tried to alibi himself with a wild story about them both being attacked by some bug-eyed monster—"

MacDougal interrupted: "You can skip that part, Glines. The driver from the motor pool told me about it on the way over."

"Yes, sir." Glines nodded tightly. "Well, anyhow, after he'd given his story to the MP's, Sergeant Bjornberg still wasn't satisfied. Under the circumstances, and all, and what with Stone acting so peculiar, he asked me to come over and talk to him. When I got here, Stone was ugly and insulting. He refused to talk to me, and insisted on going to his quarters. I was already worried about the way he was acting, so when he got so hostile I pulled a gun on him. After all"—he flushed—"we were alone here. I hadn't thought to have a guard stand by."

"And then—?"

"He attacked me. I didn't want to shoot him, of course, and he's stronger than I am. He got hold of the gun, and then called you."

MacDougal frowned; studied the floor briefly. Then, after a moment, he turned to Stone: "Well, Carl?"

Stone could feel heat rising in his face. "What do you mean, 'Well, Carl'? Glines picked a fight with me from the moment he walked into this room. He accused me of being a traitor, went through a long rigmarole about how I was to leak information on the project—"

"If you'll check his record, you'll see that I have ample reason for thinking as I do, Mr. MacDougal!" Glines broke in sharply. "He fought with the Communists in Spain. He trained troops at Yenan. He went into Yugoslavia for the OSS; served more than a year with the Partisans. He's a Communist and a traitor, I tell you—"

Of a sudden, Stone's patience ran out. Inside him, something snapped. In one long stride he closed the distance between him and Glines; caught the fat man by the coat-front. Savagely, he slapped the pudgy cheeks—once, twice, three times.

The next instant the guards were upon him—dragging him back, slamming him against the wall.

"Gentlemen!" MacDougal roared. "We'll have no more of this!" His face was beet-red, his blue eyes flashing.

With an effort, Stone slowed his breathing. "Sorry, Mac," he apologized. "I guess I just haven't had enough practice at being called a Communist."

"Nor in curbing your temper, Mr. Stone!" The base director's voice rang ice-brittle. He pivoted to the panting, ruffled Glines. "Mr. Glines, I'd diagnose your aliment as jealousy; pure and simple. If I see any more symptoms of it, it may show up on your efficiency report."

"Yes, sir, Mr. MacDougal." The fat man made jittery motions, smoothing and straightening his coat. "I'm sorry, sir. It won't happen again."

IGNORING him, MacDougal swung back to Stone. "As for you, Carl—well, I'm still in doubt."

"In doubt—?" A cold knot seemed to draw tight in the pit of Stone's stomach. Of a sudden he seemed to sense a change in his friend's manner—a strange, rising tide of latent hostility like that he'd felt in Glines and Bjornberg.

"Yes, in doubt," MacDougal's brows drew together into a shaggy hedgerow. "The dead woman, and this monster business...your accusations and violence against Glines, here...your expressed fear that Sergeant Bjornberg, one of your best friends on the base, plans to assassinate you—I don't like the sound of such talk."

Stone stood mute, not trusting himself to answer.

"Take your tale about Bjornberg," MacDougal went on. "You claim he was on guard outside this building, waiting to kill you. But it so happens that when I called the motor pool for transportation, they sent him to drive me. He'd been there ever since he brought you to this office."

The walls seemed to close in about Stone. He knew every eye in the room was upon him; knew he had to speak. "So—?" he asked at last.

MacDougal paced the floor, big knuckled hands clasped behind him.

"I don't like to do this, Carl," he said finally, "but considering the delicate nature of our work here, the high degree of secrecy surrounding our mission, I'm afraid I don't have much choice."

The cold knot in Stone's stomach drew tighter.

MacDougal ended his pacing; dropped one hip onto the corner of the desk. His tongue moved slowly back and forth along his lower lip, and his eyes stayed focused on the floor. When he spoke, his words were careful, casual.

"Did you know we'd acquired a psychiatrist since you left for Washington, Carl?" he asked.

"A psychiatrist—!" Stone burst out in spite of himself. He started forward.

A guard's restraining hand stopped him.

"Yes. She's here on a research project." The base director's eyes still studied the floor. "Supposed to be pretty good, too. Up on all the latest stuff."

Between clenched teeth Stone grated, "MacDougal, if you think I'm crazy, say so. But so help me, if you turn me over to some headshrinker, count on it that you'll regret it to your dying day!"

As, if the words were a signal, the base director's massive head came up, jaw jutting. The blue eyes, shone hard and expressionless as marbles—shone with the same, strange light that Stone had seen in Glines' and Bjornberg's.

MacDougal said, "That's all I needed, Carl: Your threats and hostility turned on me. That's the convincer that you *do* need help."

He turned to the guards: "Mr. Stone's hereby ordered to the hospital for mental tests and observation, on my responsibility.

"Take him away!"

CHAPTER THREE

DAWN. A chill, grey desert dawn that made Stone shiver beneath his blankets.

Or maybe it wasn't the cold. Maybe it was the things in his mind, the thoughts and nightmares that kept him tossing, twisting, restless. There'd been little enough sleep for him, Lord knew—fitful moments only, from which he started up

25

in wild-eyed terror, racked by aching bones and stinging cuts and the dark uncertainties that wormed insidiously through his brain.

And now, the dawn.

Fretfully, once more he squirmed and shifted—closing his eyes against the dim light, striving to find some new position that would ease the nagging restlessness that plagued him.

But the thin-padded hospital cot only creaked the louder. New lumps and knots created pressure points against his body.

With a curse, he gave it up. Rising, he shrugged on a robe and shuffled to the open window.

If he could call a window open, when it was fitted with a safety screen so heavy that a man with an axe couldn't break through it.

He laughed aloud—short, harsh, without mirth.

Outside, the base still lay bleak and silent, a hollow city with no excuse for being except The Project. The bare, regimented streets stretched deserted between their rows of characterless prefabricated housing. To the south, the tiny airstrip spread desolate, its lone helicopter strangely skeletal at this distance in the chiaroscuro of early morning.

Stone crossed to the other window, the closed one; peered west, towards the bulk of the central Project Building.

The next instant he stiffened.

For where two weeks ago the structure had loomed square and squat, now a tower rose, from its center—a tower somehow disconcertingly unique in styling, not quite like anything he'd ever seen before.

Protuberances of unfathomed purpose marred its symmetry. Catwalks rimmed it at half-a-dozen levels. Even the material of which it was constructed resembled nothing with which he was familiar.

Stoned frowned. True enough, there were plenty of things he didn't know about The Project. That was as it should be, at a base at which security measures were so vital.

Yet at the same time, it seemed strange that he'd have heard no hint as to a construction job of such proportions.

It didn't even fit in with the architectural plans. He'd seen those, and they contained no provision for a tower. None was needed. This was a development base, not a proving ground.

Of course, plans changed. New discoveries and problems necessitated new measures, new approaches.

Even new buildings.

The trouble was, so many things seemed to have changed here in the brief span of his fortnight's absence.

The attitudes and atmosphere, for instance. And the people.

People like Bjornberg and Glines and MacDougal.

Or maybe it was he that had changed, the way they said.

Maybe he was really crazy.

He was still brooding about it when the door opened.

The click of the lock took him unawares. There'd been no warning, no sound of footsteps.

Instinctively, he spun about.

Reva stood framed in the doorway.

It rocked him, hard. So hard he could only stand gaping at her cool blonde loveliness, groping for words he couldn't find.

"Good morning, Carl." Her face, her voice, were grave. Briskly, she stepped across the threshold, crisp and neat in a starched white smock, and closed the door behind her.

The spell broke. "Reva—!" he choked. "Reva, what are you doing here?"

Her manner stayed detached, impersonal. "I was assigned here nearly two weeks ago, Carl." And then: "I'm *Doctor* Adams now, you know."

"You mean—you're the psychiatrist?"

She nodded, grey eyes steady. "I'm afraid so, Carl. And I know its going to be difficult for both of us after the...personal...relationship. But I didn't have much choice, since I'm the only qualified person here. Mr. MacDougal made that rather plain."

PIN-PRICKS of rising fury seethed through Stone. "You're going along with this farce, then? You'll run me through the mill like any other screwball, in spite of everything—the way it was between us, as close as we were together?" He didn't even care that the words came out thick and angry.

The grey eyes dodged his, now. As if to cover it, Reva moved to the room's lone chair; sat down.

"Answer me!" Stone stormed. "Give it to me straight: Are you going to help them frame me?"

"No one's going to frame you, Carl. It's just that you may be...sick. That's all that I'm to check on."

A tremor crept into Reva's voice as she spoke. Hastily, she brought out a pencil and a notebook. "There'll be a few tests, that's all—Minnesota Multiphase Personality, Inventory, Rorschach, TAT, electroencephalogram, in case you're interested in the names. And I'll want to talk to you, of course—discuss these things you've done that seem to bother Mr. MacDougal and the others. There won't be anything unpleasant about it. We can work most of it out over coffee, probably."

"We'll do it straight, you mean!" Stone clenched his fists, trying to fight down the red tide of rage that surged within him. "Forget your damn coffee, Doctor Adams! I'm just one more nut to you. Quit trying to hide it!"

Reva's face went stiff. She rose quickly; stood very tall and straight. "Very well, then, Carl. We'll handle it just as you prefer. The electroencephalogram comes first. The machine's down at the end of the hall to your right. Just follow me."

High heels clicking, she left the room.

As quickly as it had flared, Stone's fury ebbed. Numbly, he stumbled down the hall after her.

What was it that held him so on edge, so close to the ragged brink of violence? The fight with the monster? The trouble with Bjornberg and Glines and MacDougal? The lack of sleep?

But no. Those were only symptoms of an ever-growing inner tension.

Yet why should he be tense? He'd seen trouble before—lots of it. Violence, too; blood by the bucket. But it hadn't affected him this way. Through all of it, he'd won a reputation as a man who thrived on situations fraught with worry and frustration. That was why they'd sent him here in the first place, to handle security problems on this base…

And to blow up at Reva, still feeling about her as he did…to let go at her, when all he could really think of was the hunger in him for her; the desire to take her, hold her, crush her to him…

Ahead of him, the heels stopped clicking. Reva pushed open a door; stepped aside. "In here please. Lie down on the couch. I'll attach the electrodes. It won't hurt a bit…"

The morning came and went, a jumble of accordion-folded graph sheets and pictures, ink blots and questions. Stone sorted cards, made up stories, drew figures, lay in black silence while electrical impulses eddied through his brain.

There was no coffee, no by-play. Reva stayed Doctor Adams. To the hilt. Lunchtime found Stone alone in his cubicle.

Thirty minutes later they were back at the tests.

But only half Stone's mind was on them.

The other half kept re-appraising Reva.

She'd changed, somehow, just like the others. Her impersonality carried a hard, suspicious edge. A dozen times—a hundred—Stone caught her eyes upon him. Not just measuring either: Cold; almost actively hostile.

Especially when she probed him with questions about the woman, and the monster.

LATE afternoon found them in her office, with Reva cross examining him about his feelings toward Glines and Bjornberg.

The implication was that he'd always hated them both; that the clashes were only the culmination of long-repressed resentment.

Stone's palms grew moist, his heart action uneven.

Of a sudden, he could take no more of it.

"Damn it, Reva!" he exploded. "They jumped me, don't you get it? They started sticking knives in me the second that they saw me!" Vaguely, he was aware that his voice had risen; that he was shouting. He didn't care. "What would you have done, damn it? How would you feel if people accused you of murder and treason to your face, when you had done nothing at all—?"

He broke off, seething.

The phone rang before Reva could speak again.

She picked up the receiver, cool and efficient, her eyes still on her notebook. "Doctor Adams speaking." A pause. "No, Mr. MacDougal, I've hardly begun, let alone finished.

These things take time." Another pause. "Yes. Yes, I have uncovered a certain amount of pertinent data. But—"

A longer pause. While Stone watched, the smooth planes and curves of Reva's face seemed to stiffen. Her fingers tightened visibly on her pencil, pressing down. The point snapped, loud in the stillness.

She said, "Very well, then, Mr. MacDougal. If you insist. —Yes, I'll be waiting in my office."

She hung up the phone.

Stone smiled thinly. "Report time?"

She didn't answer.

"I know how it is. They always push you." Stone leaned back in his chair. For no good reason, all at once he felt more in command of the situation than he had since this whole mad tangle had erupted.

Reva looked away, still saying nothing.

Stone pressed on: "It's too bad things had to work out the way they did... Between us."

Reva's eyes stayed on the wall. "We each got what we wanted." Her voice was flat, controlled. Too tightly controlled.

"Did we?" Stone grimaced. "Maybe you did. I didn't. Because I wanted you. And I didn't get you."

Was it his imagination, or did Reva's breathing quicken just a fraction?

"Being married to a security man's no cinch. I know that. It can get pretty damn worrisome and lonely, like you said when you broke it off. But right now, I'm wondering if psychiatry can't be lonely, too—"

The mask that was Reva's face drew tighter...tighter...

"—Especially if you're a woman, Reva—a woman like you, who knows what love is, and needs it—"

In a flash, like an eggshell shattering, the mask cracked and fell apart. Reva turned on him—teeth bared, eyes suddenly streaming. "Shut up!" she screamed. White knuckled, her small fist beat a convulsive tattoo on the desk's polished surface. "Shut up, I tell you! Leave me alone—alone... alone..."

Her voice died. She slumped on one arm across her notebook, face hidden. The slim shoulders shook with her sobs.

From the office doorway, MacDougal said, "That was dirty, Carl. As dirty as anything you've ever done."

Stone started. Reva gasped aloud and came erect in one swift movement, even as she turned away.

MacDougal stalked heavily to the nearest chair and sat down. Face hewn in granite, he ignored Stone; addressed Reva: "I'm sorry about this, Doctor Adams. Believe me, I wouldn't run you through such a mill for all the world, if it weren't absolutely necessary."

"It's...quite all right, Mr. MacDougal." Face almost composed once more, Reva resumed her seat. "I'll give you my tentative report as soon as the attendant returns Mr. Stone to his room." She reached towards a buzzer button.

MacDougal halted her with a gesture. His blue eyes were cold. "Don't bother, Doctor. I'm not inclined to spare Stone's tender feelings, after what he just did to you."

"It's not a matter of feelings, Mr. MacDougal." Abruptly, Reva was very much the doctor. "There's a therapeutic issue involved. And Mr. Stone's my patient."

TIGHT-LIPPED, Stone leaned forward. "Get on with it!" he clipped. "I want to hear what you've got to say as much as he does. If I'm crazy, I've got a right to know it."

"'Crazy' is hardly a meaningful term, medically speaking, Mr. Stone." Reva stared down at her notes; "However, if you insist..."

"I do."

"Very well, then." She turned to MacDougal; tapped an accordion folded graph on the desk. "Are you familiar with electroencephalography, Mr. MacDougal?"

The base director shrugged. "Only vaguely."

"Then let me begin by explaining that the electroencephalograph is a device which measures currents within the brain and records them on a chart. A trained technician can then interpret the patterns in diagnostic terms."

"I see."

"In Mr. Stone's case"—Reva studied the chart—"the electroencephalogram shows marked deviation from the norm. I'm inclined to believe that the pattern indicates he's a victim of epidemic encephalitis."

"Encephalitis—?" MacDougal frowned. "I'm afraid you'll have to explain, Doctor. I've never heard of it."

Reva nodded gravely. "That's not surprising, sir. No acute cases have been reported since 1925. The ones we see today are chronic—the aftermath of an epidemic that swept the country, beginning in 1919."

"And the results?"

"That all depends." Reva sketched meaningless patterns with her pencil. "You see, the disease wreaks havoc in the brain. There's tissue damage and, later, of course, residual lesions. Ganglion cells and neurons degenerate or disappear. Behavior difficulties often follow, too—chronic irritability, emotional instability, psychopathic conduct."

"You tell it scary," Stone said tightly. "There's just one catch, though: So far as I know, I never had any such disease."

Reva didn't look up. "I'm afraid that's easily possible, Carl. It may have run concurrently with influenza or some other sickness. Plenty of cases weren't detected. But the damage still was done."

"Then how is it I've survived? Why haven't they carted me off before now?"

"Because of the nature of the disease, Carl." For the first time, Reva faced him squarely. "You see, it can become progressive, even after months and years. When that happens…" Helplessly, she spread her hands.

A numbness crept through Stone. He slumped in his chair. The room seemed to grow dim around him. He hardly heard the things the other two were saying.

Was this to be the end for him, then? Must he live out his life walled away from the world in some mental hospital?

Again, he lived through the night before…tried to recall the way he'd felt, the things he'd done.

He'd been tired, yes; but that was to be expected, what with the long trip in. And his spirits had certainly been good enough.

Then he'd seen the woman…fought the monster.

And whether anyone believed him or not, the battle had been reality, not delusion. He had the scars to prove it.

Chronic irritability? Emotional instability? Psychopathic conduct? Those were terms that fitted Bjornberg and Glines better than they did him.

Though he had to admit he'd been on the jumpy side, ever since he'd reached the base.

Ever since he'd reached the base—!

With a rush, the pieces fell into pattern.

Last night, he'd fought a monster—a creature like nothing ever seen on earth, in hell or heaven.

The dying woman had gasped of robots on a mesa.

Bjornberg had accused him of murder.

Glines had sworn he was a Communist.

MacDougal had ordered him checked for mental aberration.

An unscheduled, other-worldish tower had risen atop the Project Building.

Reva had diagnosed him as an encephalitic, fully capable of psychopathic conduct and suitable for confinement.

He himself had developed a sudden tension so nerve shattering as to make him question his own sanity.

It all added up to just one thing: Something horribly dangerously wrong.

But not with him. No.

With the base!

But what? What could possibly account for such mad deviation?

HE looked up sharply. Reva was still talking:

"—so after your description of Carl's behavior, Mr. MacDougal, my first thought was paranoia. The systematized delusions and hallucinations tied in with it, and so did his tendency to violence. But I've given him the Rorschach test, and the TAT, and neither of them show any indication of it. So tentatively, I'm forced to fall back on encephalitis. It manifests itself so many ways—it's more polymorphic than syphilis, even…"

Systematized delusions—? Hallucinations? Stone felt a sudden, quick twinge of excitement. The behavior of the people here on the base fitted that pattern.

Yet how could a whole organization turn paranoid?

Besides, Reva had just said that he himself didn't check out for it on the tests.

Thoughtfully, he studied her.

She knew about these things, these mental twists, and she'd just come here.

Could the trouble be some strange infection she'd brought with her?

For that matter, why would a psychiatrist be assigned to a development base, anyhow?

It was an interesting question. Spontaneously, he cut in on the conversation: "Reva..."

She looked around. "Yes, Carl?"

"Just what is this research project of yours?"

Her face froze, lips half-parted. The grey eyes—it was as if shutters had suddenly slammed closed behind them.

Cold, hostile shutters.

MacDougal said quickly, "I'm afraid we'll have to bounce that one, Carl. *Verboten*. Doctor Adams' work is classified, highly confidential."

Ice hung on his words—the same kind of ice that glazed Reva's eyes.

And Glines'. And Bjornberg's.

Stone held his face immobile. "Sorry. I didn't know."

Reva had come here. Strange things had happened.

Reva was a psychiatrist. Base personnel showed something close to mental disorder.

Cause and effect?

It could bear some thought. Quite a bit of thought, in fact. Not to mention thorough investigation.

MacDougal's blue eyes had narrowed. Abruptly, he turned to Reva. "Doctor Adams, I'm afraid I've imposed on you. It's not fair to ask you to treat patients, in addition to your...other work."

Reva's slim shoulders moved a fraction. "I admit the facilities are hardly adequate, Mr. MacDougal."

"Then you recommend a mental hospital?"

"I'm afraid so."

"We'll have him flown out tonight in the helicopter, then. Right now." The base director surged to his feet. "Let's go, Carl."

Stone gripped the arms of his chair.

One wrong question—and in seconds they'd arranged to put him out of circulation.

Which meant he'd been right: There *was* a relationship between Reva's coming, her work, and the changes on the base.

Only a lot of good knowing it would do him, locked away in a back ward of some asylum. Even if he was actually all right it would take months to convince the doctors.

So much for his plans.

Unless—

"Hurry it up, Carl. This is all for your own good, you know."

Wordless, Stone arose. Carefully casual, he glanced out the nearest window.

It was almost dark.

So much the better.

He moved on into the hall and shuffled towards the detention room where he'd spent the night. Reva and MacDougal followed.

The door was locked. Stone stood aside, waiting loose-muscled while Reva inserted the key and opened the door.

"I won't keep you waiting long, Carl," MacDougal said. "We'll pick you up just as soon as I locate a pilot."

Stone drew a deep breath, "Any time." He started forward.

The base director shifted aside to let him pass.

Stone smashed down his foot with all his might on the other's instep.

MacDougal cried out...tottered off-balance.

Twisting, Stone shoved him hard against Reva. Together, the pair sprawled on the floor of the detention room.

Stone slammed and locked the door behind them. It muffled their cries most satisfactorily.

Bleak-eyed, then, he strode down the corridor and the stairs and out into the night...

CHAPTER FOUR

BASE Directory Service gave Stone both Reva's addresses—her prefab, and the building assigned her for her project.

Hanging up the phone, he pushed his way out of the crowded drugstore, then stood hesitating on the curb of the broad, bright-lighted parkway that ran round the parking center.

Home, or office? Which should it be?

He frowned.

The base alarm system blasted in the same instant.

The noisy crowd fell suddenly silent. People paused, fell back a step. Eyes shifted, searched.

The siren's shrill scream died away.

Ripples of apprehension rose on its echo. Little groups drew close together, milling aimlessly.

A tiny chill ran through Stone. He had no choice now. Distance was the vital factor, and the office address was the closest.

With an effort, he held his steps even and unhurried. Crossing the parkway, he headed south on the nearest street.

All about him, men and women were emptying from the prefabs peering this way and that talking excitedly. Off to the right, out by the Project Building motor pool, a jeep's lights flashed on. A gunned motor roared. The lights swerved north as the vehicle raced away.

Seconds later, another followed. Then another, and another.

Elsewhere, in all directions, other motors droned as the base security system came to life.

The chase was on.

Stone veered between the buildings, out of sight, then broke into a dogtrot.

A cross-street. Pausing in the shadows, he strained his eyes against the night, searching both ways for signs of the blockade the jeeps were setting up, according to plan.

It was a good plan, too; he'd helped devise it. Once the vehicles reached their stations, a rabbit couldn't move across the base undetected.

After that, there'd be a block check, certain capture.

But until then— He strode across the street, not too fast till again he reached the welcoming shadows. There, once in the darkness, he broke into a pelting run.

More cross-streets; more speed. Then the last line of prefabs.

Beyond them spread the dim expanse of the Related Projects Area, with its high wire fence and guarded gates.

Stone halted, breathing hard, and smoothed his shirt and combed his hair. Then, boldly, he strode towards the nearest point of entry.

The guard on the gate watched through the mesh, cold-eyed and silent, as he approached.

Stone said, "Message for Doctor Coughlin, Materials Research. Here's my pass."

He extended his wallet as he spoke. Cradling his rifle, the guard unlatched the gate and reached out to take it.

Stone smashed the free-swinging gate violently against him.

The guard lurched back; tried to jerk up his rifle.

Side-stepping, Stone lunged in close. Savagely, he hammered an uppercut to the other's jaw.

The guard dropped.

Ripping the man's shirt into strips, Stone bound and gagged him in seconds. Then, snatching up the rifle, he ran for the shadows.

The small, one-story brick building that housed Reva's project stood apart from its fellows, far back in an isolated corner of the Related Projects Area. A steel framework like a miniature radio tower rose close beside it, perhaps fifty feet tall.

Smashing open the locked door with the rifle-butt, Stone snapped on the lights and surveyed the place.

THE room in which he stood was a typical office. Filing cases banked one wall. A desk flanked by bookshelves stood against a second. There was a long table littered with papers and, incongruously, a small bowl of flowers. Three chairs, a water cooler, and a coat rack completed the furnishings.

Hurriedly, Stone crossed to the nearer of the two inside doors.

The first led to a washroom.

The second was locked.

Stone hesitated, a vague uneasiness upon him. It was as if the tension that rode him had been suddenly, sharply heightened. His muscles ached; his fingers showed a tendency to tremble.

The humming impinged on him, then.

It was as vague as his uneasiness—a sound that was not a sound, almost.

Stone turned slowly—straining his ears; trying to trace the murmur to its source.

Finally he placed it: It centered on the door beside which he stood.

He swung the rifle-butt. Once—twice—three times.

Lock and door stood fast.

Once again Stone hesitated. Then, reversing the rifle and standing aside to avoid a ricochet, he triggered a shot at the lock.

Metal jangled through the echo. Another blow with the butt, and the door creaked open.

The windowless room beyond, from its cramped size, had probably been planned primarily for storage.

Now, though, it overflowed with electronic equipment, from floor to ceiling a buzzing maze of tubes and condensers and coils and complicated circuits such as Stone had never seen before.

Could this machine be responsible for his uneasiness and the strange behavior on the base?

There was one sure way to find out.

Narrow-eyed, nerves atingle, he pivoted, searching for the master switch...located it at last, set at the far end of the narrow space between a transformer and the wall.

He reached out; gripped the shiny black handle.

Then, before he could throw it, a harsh voice from the office behind him snarled, "Move an inch and you're dead!"

Stone went rigid.

"Now come out! On the double!"

Stone's spine tingled. He let go the switch and slowly turned.

Colt in hand, hard-eyed and lethal, Sergeant Bjornberg stood hunched in a gunman's crouch on the far side of the office.

Glines flanked him.

Stone's lips felt stiff. Of a sudden he could feel death's hand on his shoulder.

Bjornberg moved a quick step forward. "Come out, I said!"

The smirk on Glines' fat face would have fitted a cat better. A well-fed cat, toying with a mouse.

Stone sucked in air.

"What's the matter, Mr. Stone?"

It was Glines talking now—sneering, mocking. "You took a gun away from me last night. Why don't you take the sergeant's?"

"Shut up!" rasped Bjornberg. And then, to Stone: "I said come out! Away from that equipment!"

'Away from that equipment…'

Ever so slowly, Stone let out the deep breath he'd been holding. "No, thanks, Sergeant."

"What—!" Bjornberg's finger went white on the trigger.

STONE smiled stiffly. "I said no, Joe. I'd rather let you shoot—because whether you hit me or not, that forty-five's going to tear up a lot of transistors."

Bjornberg's mouth worked. "Damn you, Stone!" And Glines came in high and shrill. "You should have hit him with the barrel from behind, Sergeant! You shouldn't have warned him!"

Ever so casually, Stone leaned back against the framework of the machine.

"I'll still take him!" Bjornberg snarled. "Here, cover me!"

He passed the Colt to Glines and started forward, hands raised in a judo fighter's guard.

Stone lunged for the switch.

This time, there was no turning back, no hesitation. He slammed the black handle down even as Bjornberg crashed against him.

The humming died in a click of circuit breakers. The tubes began to dim.

Twisting, too cramped to strike a blow, Stone grappled with Bjornberg. Together, they rocked back to the far side of the doorway, fighting with knees and teeth and elbows.

Then the sergeant broke free; leaped back, out into the office.

Instead of trying to follow, Stone spun about and smashed his foot through a device that looked like an off-beat magnetron. Clutching whole handfuls of wiring, he tore one of the upper racks of equipment out bodily.

Then Bjornberg was upon him again. The man's weight hammered him down. He caught a wicked blow in the back of the neck that sent him sagging to his knees on the floor.

Now a fist jarred his head back. Desperately, he caught one of Bjornberg's ankles and wrenched it up and around, twisting with savage force.

It was the sergeant's turn to crash to the floor. Rolling clear of him, Stone scrambled to his feet.

His adversary did likewise.

Then, as they started to circle, each searching for an opening, a voice cut through: "Carl! Sergeant! Stop it!" It was Glines, almost shouting. "Stop it, I tell you! Stop it!"

Wary, still gasping for breath, Stone drew back.

It was only then that it came to him, dazedly, that the strange tension he'd felt for the past twenty-four hours had left him. In spite of Bjornberg's blows, his head seemed clearer than it had been since the night before. His muscles no longer ached with strain. His hands had lost their tendency to tremble.

Instead of all such, now, an intense, overwhelming weariness hung upon him; nothing more.

Across from him, Bjornberg shook his head jerkily, as if to clear his brain. The hard lines had vanished from his face. Suspicion clouded his eyes no longer. They were open now, wide open, frank and friendly the way Stone had always known them.

Over by the desk, Glines shifted awkwardly, the Colt forgotten on the floor beside him. His mouth hung loose, and he looked stunned, incredulous—a fat, good-natured little man with just a bit of the old maid in him. "Carl," he mumbled, swabbing perspiration from his forehead, "Carl, what have I been doing?"

Bjornberg broke in: "Did I really say you killed that woman, Carl? My God, I must have been crazy!"

Of a sudden Stone's legs were weak as water. He stumbled to the nearest chair; slumped in it.

"This whole base has been crazy," he grunted.

Glines' pudgy hands moved nervously. He groped: "But how—I mean, what happened—?"

"It was driven crazy, that's what happened," Stone said tightly. He jerked a thumb over his shoulder. "That machine in there did it."

"The machine—?" This from Bjornberg. His broad brow wrinkled. "I thought it was a project—"

"And you thought it was important too, didn't you? Important enough to kill me for?"

The sergeant's face grew red. He shifted from one foot to the other. "I guess I did, Carl. Only now, well—damn it, I'm all mixed up!"

"Who isn't?" Stone turned to Glines. "How'd you feel—last night, when you heard about me, I mean?"

THE fat man squirmed. "It's—Carl, I don't know how to tell you…" He chewed his puffy lower lip. "As well as I can remember, I'd been feeling tight and jittery for a long time—a week or more. Then, when the sergeant woke me up and told me about you—and that dead woman—and your story about the monster—well, it was strange. All at once I was angry. I hated you, and I was afraid of you, somehow. I kept remembering all kinds of little things, and by the time I got to the office I—I knew you were a Communist. I *knew* it." Nervously, again he swabbed his forehead, scarlet now as

Bjornberg's. "I hope you understand, Carl; I just can't explain it."

"I understand, all right," Stone said grimly. "The trouble is, I can't explain it either. Not all of it. Not the important parts."

"But the machine, you said—"

"Sure, the machine did it. But why?" Stone leaned forward. "Look: First of all, somebody had to design it. Then somebody else had to approve it, order it built. Why?"

Glines shook his head helplessly. Bjornberg stared at the floor.

Stone pressed on: "Second, it didn't seem to cause any trouble—outside of making everybody jittery—till I came along. But when I did, everybody went haywire. Except me. Or maybe I did, too. Maybe I didn't really fight a monster.

"But I think I did, and I've got some scars to prove it. So that brings up a third point: Why didn't it throw me, like it did the rest of you? How is it I could figure out that something was wrong on the base, and that this project was responsible, when nobody else could?"

"It's crazy, just crazy, that's all," muttered Bjornberg.

"Maybe. But I doubt it." Stone rose stiffly. "There's somebody I want to ask some questions—" He stopped short. "Tell me this: How'd you happen to come here looking for me?"

Glines frowned. "That was my idea, Carl. Mr. MacDougal sent for me after he and Doctor Adams finally got out of that room at the hospital and sounded the alarm for you. He asked me if I had any idea where you might go—after all, I'd worked with you for a long time. At first I said I didn't know. Only then Doctor Adams made some remark about your—your condition, and said she hoped you wouldn't twist your delusions of persecution around to where you'd try to do something to her, like you'd done to that dead woman. Mr. MacDougal said she didn't need to worry about it, that he'd see that she got home all right, and they left. But the more I thought about what she'd said, the more sense it made, and I began to wonder if you might not try to sneak out here and booby-trap the building. Finally, the thought of it got to worrying me so much that I called Sergeant Bjornberg and came out here with him." Glines paused, laughed self-consciously. "It sounds silly now, doesn't it? But at the time nothing in the world seemed so important as to make sure nothing happened to Doctor Adams or her project."

Reva. Always, it came back to Reva.

"Good enough," Stone said. Tight-lipped, he started for the door.

"Where you going?" Bjornberg demanded.

Stone held his voice flat and level. "To see Doctor Adams."

"That figures," the sergeant nodded. "We even got a jeep back by the next building to take you to her."

"Besides," Glines chimed in, opening the door, "you'll need us to pass you through the blockade."

He started down the outside steps.

The next instant, his wild scream of terror split the night.

CHAPTER FIVE

FOR Stone, that moment lasted a thousand years.

Then it was over, Glines' shriek dying.

The horrid spell broke. He lunged for the door, Bjornberg on his heels.

But something smooth and slippery brushed his face as he crossed the threshold. Instinctive panic flaring in him, he threw himself sidewise.

Before he could hit the ground, rubbery tentacles swept about him. In a black delirium of movement, he found himself caught up and lifted; crushed close to a gelid, barrel-like body.

Desperately, he tried to twist free, fight clear. But a dozen discs clung to him with vicious suction. Every move he made seemed to draw the tentacles tighter—crushing him; squeezing the very breath from his body.

Now one had looped about his throat, a living rope to cut the blood off from his brain. Glines' screams seemed dim and far away. The sky held too many stars...

Then thunder rocked the night—the thunder of a heavy Colt, fired at close range.

For the fraction of a second, the tentacles hold relaxed. Stone's feet touched the ground. Tearing his throat free, he gulped in a tremendous, sobbing breath.

"Joe!" he shouted. "Joe, shoot for the band, the belt—"

Nightmare-like, in the same instant the tentacles once again constricted. He had no more breath, not for shouting, nor for breathing either.

But the Colt roared like an echo, so close now that the powder-fumes stung Stone's nostrils. The monster's barrel-body rocked under hammer-blows of impact. Fluid spilled across Stone's legs in a chilling gush.

Then he was free, falling, slammed to the gravel. Tentacles writhed across him in a rush.

Rolling, Stone lurched up.

The monster that had held him now clutched Bjornberg. In a raging frenzy, its tentacles swung the sergeant high into the air wrenching at his body. His head lolled loose, horribly disjointed.

Then, with cataclysmic violence, the thing hurled him from it. He crashed against the brick wall of the building;

spilled down in a crumpled heap beside a sodden form that could only be Glines' body.

Stone turned and ran.

Ahead of him, a second monster swept out from behind the building.

Stone kept to his course, straight at the thing. If asked, he could not have told why. Perhaps it was bravado, perhaps desperation.

Or perhaps pure madness.

The creature hesitated, its tentacles flickering in a way that was almost startled. Then, abruptly, it drew back, as if suddenly wary—not quite certain of Stone's potential.

Beyond it, the jeep loomed. Stone made it in a final rush; vaulted into the driver's seat. Kicking the motor to life, he wheeled the vehicle around in a screaming curve, jammed the accelerator to the floor, and raced for the main gate.

In seconds, the entrance came into view. Stone started to apply the brakes.

But the gate stood open. No guards appeared to challenge his exit.

Beyond the fence, the street stretched bare and empty, with no sign of blockading troops.

Stone bore down on the gas once more. He still didn't dare to pause to think; not yet. The horror still clung too close. Too many things hung unexplained.

Things like why the firing back at Reva's project building hadn't drawn a half-track full of guards. Why the gate stood open. Why the streets were empty, the housing units dark.

But such were trivia; they could wait. He only knew his friends were dead, and what he had to do.

Number Ten Q Street, Northeast. Reva's prefab.

But no light in the windows.

STONE spun the jeep right at the next corner; headed back west towards the Central Project Building, with its bright lights and strange new tower.

Then, ahead, a white-striped barrier caught his lights. It blocked the street.

Stone braked the jeep.

Half-a-dozen soldiers stood grouped to one side of the crossbar. Before Stone could even speak, two of them hurriedly slung their rifles, moved the barrier out of the way, and waved him on. They made no move to halt or check him.

The area beyond looked like a full-scale military operation—barricades, barbed wire, sandbagged strong points, machine guns.

Hands slick on the jeep's wheel, still not daring to ask questions, Stone maneuvered his vehicle through the narrow corridor left open.

He reached the fence that circled the Central Project Area…passed through the gate.

On the other side, thronging civilians milled and muttered. A single word, rising from a thousand throats, pulsed at him wave-like:

"Monsters…monsters…monsters…monsters…"

Of a sudden, Stone understood it all—the barricades, the darkened houses; the open gates, the lack of questions.

New chills ran through him. He cursed the icy sweat that drenched his body.

Slowed by the crowd, the jeep was more hindrance now than help. Abandoning it, Stone pushed his way towards the square, squat block of the Central Project Building.

A private with rifle and fixed bayonet barred the entrance. A corporal sang out. "Hold it, Mister!"

Stone said tightly, "You hold it—if you want to take the responsibility. I've got information about this business."

A lieutenant moved up. "Talk ahead, Mister. I'll listen."

"I'll talk—to the base director. And he's the only one."

The lieutenant's eyes narrowed. "What's your name, Mister?"

"Carl Stone."

"Carl Stone—!" Visibly, the officer stiffened. He shoved the private aside; elbowed back the corporal. "Come on, then! What are you waiting for?"

In seconds, they were at the door of MacDougal's second-floor office.

The base director sat hunched over his desk, snapping hard, clipped words into a phone. His broad face looked drawn and haggard, and the hand with which he pushed back his stiff, greying hair seemed not too steady.

Stone's gaze flicked to Reva Adams.

She occupied a chair in one corner. Only in the faint shadows beneath her eyes did she show any trace of the tension that radiated from the base director. For the rest, she was as always—sleek, lovely, all woman, her blonde hair swept smoothly back and falling to her shoulders, her firm body filling out the silken sheath of her dress.

Even the sight of her sent fury surging through Stone. Pushing past the lieutenant, he stalked into the room. "Hang up that phone, Mac. You've got company."

Reva jerked in her chair. Her hand flew to her throat.

The base director's massive head came around sharply. He started up from his seat. "Carl—!"

"Right. Alive and breathing."

There was no good humor in the words, the way Stone said them. He heeled shut the door, closing out the lieutenant.

"Carl, we thought you were dead—"

"I'm not blaming you, Mac. Not you." Stone jerked his head towards Reva. "Her, I'm not so sure of."

"Doctor Adams—?" MacDougal stared at him blankly. "What do you mean, Carl?"

"I mean I've found out the nature of her project." Grimly, Stone pivoted to face the woman. "How about it, Reva? What's the explanation for that electronic brain-trap I found out in your building?"

Her slim hands moved nervously in her lap. Her eyes dodged his. "I—I don't know what you mean."

"You don't?" Stone made an elaborate business of surprise. And then, slashing out, hard and savage: "I'll tell *you*, then. I'm talking about that transmitter you had locked in your storeroom—that humming, buzzing little devil-ma-chine that kept this whole base half-crazy till I smashed it!"

MacDougal's heavy fist hammered on the desk. "Damn it, Carl! Talk sense!"

"I am talking sense—the only sense anybody's heard around here in the past two weeks!" Stone roared him down. "Has it occurred to you that you feel a little differently about me now than you did a couple of hours ago?"

THE base director suddenly looked sheepish. "Oh, that—" He groped vaguely. "I—well, I don't know what got into me, Carl. Nervous strain, maybe. The pressure of sweating out the big project, here; all the worry, the being afraid it wouldn't work out right."

"And then, awhile ago, all of a sudden you knew that it was foolish, didn't you? That I wasn't crazy, or a traitor, or a murderer, or anything else except what I'd always been?"

"Well—well, yes." MacDougal brushed perspiration from his chin. "As soon as I got back here, and stopped to think it over—"

"You mean, as soon as I smashed that machine! Bjornberg, Glines—they both snapped out of the fog when I did it, right before my eyes."

"Glines? Bjornberg?" MacDougal's head came up. "I've had a call out for them. Where are they?"

Tight-lipped, Stone fought down the wave of sickness that rose in him. "They're dead, Mac. Dead. Killed by the monsters that everybody claimed I didn't see."

"Dead..." Face sagging, the base director slumped into his chair.

"I'm as sorry as you are, Mac. But that's not enough." Stone pushed in, driving his words hard. "What's important is now, the living. They're the ones we've got to think about."

"Yes. Of course." MacDougal's voice still echoed dull and empty.

"So the first point's to get it across that I'm not crazy, that I'm telling the truth: Last night, that transmitter out at Reva's building wouldn't let you believe me. Then, when I smashed it, and everybody snapped back to normal, the monsters came—so many of them that you've had to clear the base, move all personnel into the Central Project Area for protection."

"But how—?"

"How do the monsters tie in with the transmitter, you mean?" Stone shook his head curtly. "I wouldn't know. But I'm going to find out. Our good friend Doctor Adams is going to tell us all about it."

He turned towards her chair. It was empty.

Stone went numb inside; spun about by reflex.

The office door stood an inch ajar. Reva was gone.

MacDougal cursed, surged up from his seat. "Come on!" Like a raging grizzly, he charged across the office and out into the hall.

Stone started to follow. Then, braking, he whirled and jumped to the window. Savagely, he jerked it open and thrust out his head.

Off to the right, below him, Reva was walking briskly out the building's main entrance, a picture of calm, cool poise.

Stone clutched the sill; looked down.

A soldier wearing an MP brassard stood directly beneath him. Stone shouted, "You, soldier! MP! Get that woman!"

The man looked up, startled; then to the right, following Stone's frantic gesture.

But the words had reached Reva, too. She swung round in mid-stride, her eyes wide with panic.

The MP galloped towards her. Whirling, she fled right-away from her pursuer; off towards the corner of the building.

Stone ran for the hall, only to crash into MacDougal, returning.

The base director's face was flushed. He was panting. "I couldn't find her, Carl—"

"Forget it. She's trapped. Just wait in your office." Stone headed for the stairs at a dead run.

Outside at last, then, he spotted the MP.

The man waved and gestured.

Stone went limp with relief. The soldier had Reva gripped firmly by the arm.

Stone started towards them.

Only then, suddenly, out in the open area in front of the building, a civilian gave a startled cry and pointed skyward.

Simultaneously, a high, shrill drone pulsed through the night, louder every second.

Stone looked up, sharply.

OVERHEAD, pinpoints of light were sweeping down in tight formation, converging on the Central Project Area. Lower they raced, and lower, wheeling in a spiral that would have been the envy of any jet.

Out in the crowd, a woman screamed hysterically. A man whirled, sprinting for cover.

In an instant, panic swept through the multitude like a living thing. Shrieking, bolting, clawing, civilians and soldiers alike fled in all directions.

Heart pounding, Stone pressed flat against the building.

Now one of the lights peeled off from the formation. Bullet-fast, it lanced towards the spot where Stone stood, so low that it almost seemed to skim the ground.

He drew a quick, shallow breath, with the feeling that it must surely be his last.

Only then the thing spun into an arc, bare yards away from him. For an instant it hovered almost motionless, barely three feet in the air, before riding a beam of purple flame from its base down to the ground.

Stone could see it better now. A tripod of tall, thin metal legs supported a blocky central unit that vaguely resembled a cake ice-cream cup with a broad lip flaring at the top. Light glinted from three eye-like protuberances set close against the brim.

While Stone watched, the purple beam that speared down from the center of the body unit turned scarlet, then dazzling pink. At the same time, two funnel-shaped appendages detached themselves from the base and darted out, cobra-like, in either direction along the building's wall on slender tentacles of cable.

Off to Stone's right, a shout rang out. Then a shot.

He turned just in time to glimpse the tentacle flick out like a whiplash at the MP who'd captured Reva. Its funnel-shaped end struck him in the chest—a blow so violent that even Stone could hear it hit.

The man staggered back; sank to the ground.

Paying him no heed, the cable flipped high into the air, coiling as it rose.

Then, writhing like a living thing, it was descending…slapping down at Reva Adams.

Her scream rang wild and ragged. Like one possessed, she darted out from the building, blonde hair streaming.

Deftly, the cable-coil shifted, pulling tight even as it dropped its loop around her.

Tripping, she plunged to the ground.

In spite of himself, without volition, Stone lunged towards her. Unreasoning panic roweled him with razor spurs.

Almost as if timing itself to his charge, the cable-tentacle threw another loop around the struggling, screaming woman, then it swept her high into the air, well above Stone's head just as he reached the spot where she had lain.

Desperately, he leaped straight up, clawing desperately for the cable.

Snake-like, it writhed out of reach, leaving him to fall back cursing on the gravel.

Now he saw the other tentacle's destination.

And its victim.

It was MacDougal.

The funnel-like cable-end had suckered onto his great chest and dragged him bodily out his office window. Now, still at second-story level, heedless of his struggles, the line itself twisted and looped about him half-a-dozen times, binding him tight.

Simultaneously, the flame-jet from the strange robot's base deepened to its original purple.

As the color changed, the weird craft lifted, higher into the air, and higher. Already, it had begun to pick up its characteristic spiral motion.

In the same instant, the other robots swept down, still in their tight formation. The shrill drone of the sound they gave forth welled ear-splitting, deafening.

Smoothly, the unit that had landed then resumed its place within the pattern, it's sagging prisoners hugged against it.

As one, the robots soared away, out across the encircling desert till light and sound alike were swallowed in the night.

CHAPTER SIX

THE moment that followed the flying robots' departure stretched endlessly, Seconds ticked by with Stone barely aware that they were passing. He could only stand there in mute, helpless frustration, staring up at the sky where the cones had vanished.

Out of the night they had come; into that same night they had retreated.

Only there was more to it than that.

Because they'd taken Reva and MacDougal with them. That, obviously, had been the whole purpose of their raid.

Nor had their victims gone willingly. No one who had seen those blanched, fear-stricken faces could believe they had.

No. If there'd been a plot—if Reva had really helped the monsters by setting up the transmitter at her project building—then that plot had now reversed itself, gone sour.

It was a mad twist—shattering; mind-shaking.

And it forced a whole new orientation.

For Stone, it was suddenly more than he could take or grasp. He slumped against the wall; buried his face in his hands.

Then, from all directions, sound rose and swept in and impinged upon him—a hoarse babble of voices that echoed overtones of panic.

He let his hands fall; looked up and out.

The teeming mass of humanity crammed into Central Project Area seethed like churned water. Shouts of rage rang out…roars of indignation, women's high-voice protests, the fear-straught cries of frightened children.

While Stone watched, the troops drew in to form a tight, bayonet-bristling cordon about the Project Building, thrusting the civilians back.

Numb, drained, Stone turned from the scene and made his way to the main entrance.

A half-track stood drawn up close by it, with a lieutenant colonel barking orders into a radiophone. Pausing, Stone listened long enough to ascertain that the man was talking to the commander of an armored unit on maneuver somewhere out in the desert—calling it in to reinforce the troops stationed at the base in case of further robot raids or incursions by the monsters.

Chaos, Unlimited.

Shaking his head wearily, Stone went on into the building and headed for the first-floor snack bar. The place was deserted, save for a little knot of research men who sat talking animatedly at a table beside a blaring radio at the far end of the room.

In spite of himself, Stone's lips twisted wryly. Leave it to Research. Let Earth itself collapse, and its intellectual stalwarts would still forget panic in their eagerness to argue the dynamics of the breakup.

The girl at the coffee urn gave him a wan smile. "Coffee, Mr. Stone?"

"Jug of black," Stone grunted. "I need something to help me do some thinking."

STILL talking, two of the research men came up behind him while he waited.

"…that confounded tower, that's what gets me," the first was saying. "With MacDougal gone, what do we do about it?"

"Then what Crawford said's true? Nobody except MacDougal actually knows the purpose of it?"

"You're so right. I was there when he gave the orders on it, a week-and-a-half ago. He was so excited he could hardly keep his pants on; but when Grimorski asked him what the idea was, he just stuck out his eyebrows and told Grim to mind his own business."

The second man whistled. "It puts us on a spot, then, doesn't it?"

"Spot's hardly the name for it. That tower doesn't tie in with The Project at all, except maybe for using some of the big equipment."

The girl at the coffee urn handed Stone his cup and jug. Mechanically, he took them, paid her, and stepped back out of the way of the research men.

But his mind was racing, groping. He made no move to find a table.

"One with cream and one without," the second research man told the girl. And then, speaking again to his companion: "I was talking to Santos about it. He says the only thing he can figure it for is some kind of king-size electrolytic cracker. Only it's too big to make sense, and it'd have to work on some off-beat principle that doesn't tie in with accepted theories on ionization."

"Even if it did, what would the monstrosity decompose? The atmosphere?" This from the first man. "No; I can't buy that, Dawes. If you ask me, it doesn't do anything at all."

"Oh, now, don't push those snap judgments of yours too far, Quinn." The second man looked half-worried, half-amused. "After all, why would MacDougal order the thing built, if it didn't have some function?"

"What's the obvious answer?" the man called Quinn snorted. "Our base director's cracked, that's all. The strain got too much for him. He saw how things were going on

The Project—that it just wasn't going to work out, even if it was his idea and his baby. He simply couldn't take it. So, he compensated by coming up with a new super-secret brainstorm that's as nutty as a Rube Goldberg invention."

The other research man frowned. "You really think so?"

"What else is there to think? Can you come up with any other explanation?"

"But MacDougal—damn it, Quinn, he's outstanding, brilliant—"

"The smarter they are, the wider they split. It's happened before. A man stakes his career on a job; oversells an idea. Then it falls flat. He sees his whole scientific reputation flying out the window. Unless he's mighty stable, the next stop's Bellevue."

Cups in hand, the two research men started to move away, back to their table.

For the fraction of a second, Stone hesitated. Then, abruptly, he stepped forward. "Pardon me."

The pair halted. The first man half-turned. "What—?"

Stone said, "I'm Carl Stone. Security. I couldn't help overhearing—"

The second man flinched visibly, slopping his coffee. His thin face paled a trifle.

His companion stood steady. "Go ahead." His voice was cool, not too friendly.

Stone made a placatory gesture.

"Believe me, I'm not trying to give you trouble. There'll be no nonsense about reporting anybody, no matter what. But some strange things have happened on this base lately. I need information—and maybe you two are the ones who can give it to me." He nodded to the nearest table. "How about letting me have five minutes, over coffee?"

"I've got nothing to hide. What I said's for the record." The first man stepped to the table, dropped into a chair.

The second followed, less enthusiastically.

STONE filled his cup from the jug and leaned back, hunting for the right words. "You think there's a possibility that The Project's a failure?" he asked finally.

"Possibility, my eye. It's a thousand percent certain." The first man, the one called Quinn, stirred in sugar. "Has been, for nearly a month now. But MacDougal won't give up. Because he doesn't know it? No; it's because he's scared to."

Stone frowned at Dawes. "You agree?"

The man stared down into his coffee. "I'm afraid so."

"Then why hasn't it been reported—to Washington, I mean?"

"That's—that's the base director's responsibility."

"And this other business? The tower?" Stone spoke to Quinn, this time.

"You've got me there, mister."

The man made a business of shrugging. "I've screamed loud enough about it, but no one would listen. I guess they think griping's just a habit with me, on account of my encephalitis."

Stone stiffened... *Encephalitis—?"*

"A brain disease. I picked it up in the flu epidemic of 1918, when I was a kid. Doesn't bother my thinking, but I'll admit it short-circuits my disposition sometimes."

"So—"—with difficulty, Stone held his voice level—"so, you didn't think much of the tower?"

"That's right. I didn't. But everyone else was so hipped on it they wouldn't listen—even Dawes, here, had the bug. For better than a week, they all went around acting like it was the hottest thing since blondes were invented, and the most important, even when in the next breath they'd have to admit they didn't know what it was supposed to do or how it worked. I was the only one in the place who wouldn't join their club, I think they'd have fired me, if they'd had a replacement. As it was, the supervisor just swore I was crazy and let it go at that."

"I see." Stone gripped his cup between his palms, trying to hide his hands sudden trembling.

Slowly, slowly, the pieces were falling into place.

Two weeks ago, more or less, Reva Adams had been assigned to research a mysterious project at this base.

Shortly thereafter, the transmitter at her building had gone into action.

Immediately, the thinking of the entire body of personnel had grown distorted—as witness MacDougal's order to build an apparently useless tower in the face of The Project's alleged failure.

Then he, Carl Stone, had returned—and the transmitter hadn't affected him, save to make him abnormally tense and irritable and nervous.

Reva had diagnosed him as an encephalitis victim.

And now, in Quinn, he'd discovered another encephalitic—and apparently Quinn's thinking hadn't been distorted by the transmitter, either! He'd retained his judgment, his ability to analyze and reason, in spite of admitted irritability and tension.

In other words, whatever else the transmitter might have none, it hadn't been able to influence encephalitic intellects.

Why?

Staring at his cup, Stone pondered.

"There's tissue damage," Reva had said, *"and, later, of course, residual lesions. Ganglion cells and neurons degenerate or disappear."*

That meant that the functioning of the brain was changed, impaired.

The transmitter at Reva's project building pulsed out waves that distorted the thinking of normal brains.

But encephalitics didn't have normal brains. The disease destroyed cells, burned out synapses.

So, in them, the transmitter merely heightened tension. Scar tissue slashed gaps its impulses couldn't bridge.

OF A sudden Stone felt better, than he had in days. This discovery—it was a step forward; a long, long step.

The only trouble was, he still had so far to go.

For instance, where did the monsters fit into the picture?

The robots?

How did they link to the transmitter?

And—the thought came in spite of all his efforts to shut it out—to Reva?

Because there *was* a link. There had to be. The problem was only to establish the chain of logic.

He took another sip of coffee; spoke as much to himself as to his companions: "First, I smashed the transmitter. Then, the monsters came—"

"The monsters—?" The thin faced Dawes hunched forward eagerly, seeming glad for the sudden change of subject. "I haven't heard anything about a transmitter. But these monsters—now there's something I can get my teeth in!"

"You can have 'em," Quinn grunted sourly. "Me, I wouldn't get my teeth in a monster if I was starving."

"No kidding, Quinn! I just wish I'd have seen one!" Dawes' brown eyes sparkled. "They're aliens, obviously—extraterrestrials from some other planet. Also, they've mastered space travel—which means they're superior to humans, no matter what they look like. Look how they handled the business with the robots—kidnapping our base director as a hostage, along with a psychiatrist to give 'em a hand at figuring out our mental mechanisms. Personally, I don't think there'd have been any trouble with them whatever, if people hadn't panicked. But when those women out in the prefabs saw 'em—all tentacles and whatnot—everybody stopped thinking. The troops didn't do any good, either. The aliens didn't have any choice but to fight back, once the lead started flying..."

The monsters. The tentacles.

The dead woman. Glines. Bjornberg.

Without avail, Stone tried to black out the picture. In spite of himself, he shuddered.

He knew, then, that for him there could never be any compromise with the strange creatures. No matter what he should learn, regardless of any answers the future might uncover, he could never hope to throw off his horror. His memories were too black, too bitter.

Dawes was still talking: "...and I wonder how many of us have ever stopped to consider the functional aspects of multiple tentacles. Just think how handy it'd be to have suction cups on the ends of your fingers! It's as great an evolutionary development as the thumb! And there's the business of having the tentacles on both ends of the body, too—your feet get tired, so you turn upside down and walk on the other end. The stripe around the middle is probably a sensor band—a continuous nerve unit that sees, hears, tastes, smells; that is, assuming they have our senses. Or maybe they ingest their food from the air, by osmosis, the way a frog does water—"

The flow of words showed no signs of stopping. All at once, Stone could take no more. He had to be alone, to think.

Abruptly, he rose. "Quinn, Dawes—I want to thank you both," he interrupted. "You've been a big help—more than you know."

He started to turn.

As he did so, the blaring radio down by the other occupied table went into a sudden, crackling spasm, then fell silent.

A coffee-drinker rose, reached for the dials.

But before he could touch them, the radio blared again. A voice spoke—a strange, metallic voice like none that Stone had ever heard:

"Base! Development base called Las Crescentes! I speaking to you!"

Stone went rigid. Chairs scraped at the other table.

"Listen, Base! I speaking!"

THE man who had risen from the far table twisted the volume dial.

"Listen, Base! Listen, Base! Listen, Base..." The level of the strange voice stayed constant.

The man moved the selector.

The voice came in on all bands.

The man stumbled back, white-faced and shaking. An icy finger ran up and down Stone's spine.

The clanging, harsh, metallic voice went on:

"Listen, Base! I here at World Earth from world you not know. I get element you call krypton. Must have. Take out you air. Not hurt."

Stone groped. "Krypton—?"

Quinn speaking: "Inert gas, one part in six or seven hundred thousand in normal atmosphere."

The voice again: "Must have! Take! You help, I not hurt."

"Aliens!" Dawes' nails scraped the table. "I was right! I was right!"

The voice: "Tower take. You run. Must have!"

"'Tower take'?" Quinn's eyes narrowed. "My God! You don't suppose—"

"Listen, Base—!"

64

A pause. Then, a new voice on the speaker, deep and familiar.

MacDougal's voice, thick with tension.

"John MacDougal speaking."

Stone gripped the back of his chair so hard his knuckles ached.

MacDougal: "As you've probably guessed, our visitors tonight, are from—elsewhere. Another planet. Maybe even another solar system. I'm not quite sure. There's a problem in communication. They don't have anything like what we'd term normal speech apparatus. They'd tried to get around it with the mechanical substitute you just heard, but it's pretty limited."

A pause, vibrant with nerve shattering silence.

"Anyhow, they want krypton. Why, I don't know. They just keep saying 'Must have!'"

Another pause, longer this time.

Stone's muscles were knotting.

"This krypton—we're to get it for them." MacDougal sounded old and frightened now. "They've even equipped us to do the job. It seems they've—been around quite a while. A couple of weeks, anyhow. So they did a little mind control work on one of our people, Doctor Reva Adams. Again, I don't quite know how; probably they're telepaths—maybe that's how they communicate with each other. In any case, they maneuvered things so she set up a transmitter that induced what amounted to a mild paranoia in all base personnel." A short laugh, more panic than mirth. "Including me, the base director..."

With an effort, Stone twisted the chair about and sat down. Within him, the tension kept climbing. If it went on—wildly, he wondered if a man could feel his own sanity slipping away...

MacDougal again, sounding more like himself this time: "Sorry, friends. I'm all right, and so is Doctor Adams. Just chalk up any breaks I make to nerves…" He spoke less jerkily now. His voice came through the radio's amplifier strong and steady.

STONE'S tension ebbed a fraction. He leaned forward, concentrating on the base director's every word:

"…I spoke of paranoia. As you may know, the disorder's marked by systematized delusions and hallucinations. In my own case, these centered on a conviction that I'd developed a new and revolutionary approach to The Project. Backing it up, I ordered construction of the equipment that now occupies the tower on top of the Central Project Building. In turn, the rest of you fell into a pattern that blocked off any questioning of my judgment, and built up resistance— extreme hostility, in fact—to any thought or suggestion that might threaten the work or the aliens.

"Actually, of course, my 'new development' had nothing whatever to do with The Project. On the contrary. The only function the device has is to extract krypton from the atmosphere as fast and efficiently as possible. How it works, I can't say; the design's so different from anything we know that I'm inclined to think it's based on scientific principles completely outside our experience.

"Some of you may wonder why these aliens picked our base as a place to set up their operation. Apparently there were two reasons: First, The Project involved materials and a good deal of hard-to-fabricate equipment that they needed for their krypton extraction process. Second, Las Crescentes is isolated. Their mind-control transmitter blanketed us without overlapping into any other inhabited areas, so they didn't have to worry about outside interference.

"That brings up another point: These creatures have a wave-shielding device that tops anything we know. That's how they cut in on your radios with this broadcast. It also blocks off your transmitters and telephone equipment, so don't waste time trying to get outside help.

"Getting back to the other aspects of the situation, this is the way it stacks up: If everything had gone according to plan, we'd have finished the extraction unit in the tower, drained Earth's atmosphere of krypton, and delivered it to these aliens. Probably we wouldn't t even have realized what we'd done till after they'd left the planet.

"Fortunately or unfortunately, though, something went wrong. One of our base security men, Carl Stone, was in Washington when these creatures moved in. Last night he got back. For some reason neither the aliens nor I can quite figure out, the paranoia transmitter didn't affect him. He recognized that something was wrong on the base, and he wouldn't be pressured into letting it slide. In less time than seems possible, he located the transmitter and smashed it.

"The moment the transmitter went off, the aliens knew something was wrong. They moved in on the base.

"Our troops stopped that, fast. The aliens saw they'd have to fight a pitched battle to take over. They drew back instead. Maybe they're humanitarians. Or maybe they were afraid the tower might be wrecked if shooting started. I don't know.

"Anyhow, they sent the flying robots for Doctor Adams and me. We're hostages—interpreters, I gather.

"That brings up the reason I'm talking. I'm supposed to tell you what they want you to do.

"It's simple enough: Just finish the krypton extractor according to plan just as fast as possible—they figure twenty-four hours ought to do the job.

"Then, put it into operation. They'll supply cylinders to store the krypton.

"Once it's aboard their ship, they'll turn Doctor Adams and me loose and be on their way to wherever they're going.

"They want me to hit it hard that this won't cost us anything. To us, krypton's just an inert gas, with no practical value. To them, for some reason, it's vital. They say they'll even pay us off for it by giving us whatever scraps of scientific information they've got that we're capable of absorbing.

"On the other hand—"—now MacDougal's voice developed the faintest of tremors—"—if we don't go along a hundred percent, they promise immediate, utter and complete destruction of the base, and extermination of all personnel after which, they'll pick another site for their plant and try again."

The base director paused, then; hesitated, fumbled while the silence echoed.

In the snack bar, tension climbed and eddied like a thermal updraft. Stone could hear the harsh rasp of his companions breathing.

For his own part, he dared not even suck in air, for fear his self control would crack.

"I guess that's all," MacDougal said at last. Again, as at the beginning, his voice suddenly sounded old and frightened. "I'm in no position to try to influence your decision. I don't have the right to tell you what to do, or how to do it. Make up your own minds and—and good luck—"

He broke off. Once more, the silence echoed.

Then, like a thunder-clap, the alien's clanging, metallic voice cut in—harsh, savage: "Listen, Base! I speaking! Get krypton! Must have!

"Get krypton—or die!"

The radio went dead...

CHAPTER SEVEN

FEAR stalked the base. It hung in the air...seeped through the hush...showed in trembling hands and on strained faces.

Stone felt it, too. Fear and something else.

Something that crawled and gnawed and ached within him. Something that reached out spidery tendrils to the farthest cell of his very being.

It came out in a name, pulsing in his brain: Reva...Reva...Reva...

He paced the night, hour after hour. But nowhere, nohow, could he escape her. Misty and wraithlike her face swayed before him. The soft curve of her cheek, the scent of her hair, the taste of her lips—they wouldn't leave him alone.

Her eyes were the worst: Gentle grey eyes, imploring...

He cursed aloud in the stillness.

Only there was nothing he could do. Nothing.

Seething, he sought out the headquarters.

A young captain looked up as he entered.

Stone said, "Well? What's the decision?"

"Decision?" The officer shrugged. "We're still waiting. That tank unit's coming. We got through to it before the bugs clamped down their wave-shield."

"But Doctor Adams—MacDougal—"

"The base comes first. We can't risk it—not just for two prisoners."

Stone choked harsh words off unspoken. Pivoting, he strode back out into the darkness.

A whole base, versus two prisoners.

Calculated risk, and the greatest good of the greatest number.

The commandant's attitude made sense. Of course it did.

Except for one thing:

One of the prisoners was Reva.

Only that was individual, personal, a pain deep inside him. The commandant didn't know about that. And even if he did, he couldn't afford to let it matter.

The answer? Stone scuffed at the gravel. That was the trouble: There just wasn't any answer.

Or was there?

Suppose you reversed the equation, turned the figures upside down.

The commandant saw two lives against thousands. That was his duty.

But for him, Carl Stone, it was different. He had one life; that was all.

One life, to gamble for two. His own neck to risk, on the off chance that he might save MacDougal and Reva.

It was a good thought. It made the odds look different.

Stone laughed abruptly. Who was he kidding? The odds didn't matter, nor even MacDougal. Reva was the one who counted, and Reva only.

Because he loved her. In spite of everything, he loved her.

It was decision.

Stone's breathing quickened. All at once he felt alive again, no longer numb or bowed down. The years, the bitterness, the heartbreak—like shackles struck off, as one they fell away. Cool, purposeful, his stride firm, he struck out towards the Central Project Area's main gate.

The weary guards waved him by on the strength of his security pass. Beyond the last barrier, then, he broke into a dogtrot and stayed with it all the way to the administration building lot where his car was parked.

One brief detour, to his quarters to pick up a thirty-eight. Then out onto the highway, heading east towards the spot where he'd watched the woman die.

The sky was greying now, along the horizon far ahead; another day aborning, out of the chill shadows of a desert dawn.

Bleakly, Stone wondered if he'd live to see it end.

Then tire-churned gravel marked the turn-off point. Slowing to low gear, Stone wrenched the steering wheel around and bumped off the road, out across the shoulder into the open desert.

THE trail the woman had left proved surprisingly easy to follow, still—a broken creosote bush here, kicked-over clumps of fishhook cactus there, ground shoe-scraped in between.

The tracks pointed to a high, rocky tableland perhaps three miles back from the road.

What was it the dying woman had said—"robots beyond the mesa"—?

The back of Stone's neck prickled.

His car gave out less than three quarters of a mile from the road, ambushed by rocks and a mesquite tree.

Stolidly, Stone abandoned it and set out on foot. The trail, at first so clear, had vanished now, so he set his course for the mesa and hoped for the best.

Slowly, the sun edged up. The day began to warm.

Stone plodded on, dodging cactus and keeping a sharp eye out for snakes.

He was nearly to the hill when he heard the helicopter. Before he could find a place to hide, it was hovering directly overhead...settling slowly, rotor whishing.

Hastily, Stone slid his gun out of sight beneath his coat and stood waiting.

Landing on a nearby patch of open ground, the whirlybird's pilot threw open the door. "Hey, you!"

"Yes?" Stone picked his way toward the craft. "What is it?"

The pilot scowled. "You're out of bounds. I got orders to come out and pick you up. The CO's taking no chances of getting those bugs stirred up till he knows just where we stand."

"I might have known that gate-guard would say something about me." Stone managed a rueful smile. "Well, so goes it…"

He clambered into the helicopter not even protesting; closed the door. The pilot manipulated the controls. The engine roared. Slowly, the 'copter rose, straight up into the air.

Stone reached beneath his coat. Not even bothering to speak, he brought out the thirty-eight and leveled it at the other's side.

"Hey!" The pilot stiffened. "Put that thing away. You want to get into trouble?"

"I'm already in it, friend," Stone said gently. "I might as well go whole hog." He gestured with the revolver's muzzle. "Let's have a look on the other side of that mesa."

Muttering, the pilot sent the helicopter higher.

Only then, before they had more than reached the edge of the tableland, a sound bore in upon them…a high, shrill, droning sound…

It was Stone's turn to stiffen.

Swiveling in his seat, he peered out, searching.

Beyond the mesa, a flight of the flying robots climbed into view in a swift, tight spiral, swirling up and around straight into the morning sun.

Simultaneously, the pilot exclaimed, "Look—! The tanks!"

Stone strained his eyes.

Far off in the eastern desert, tiny beetle-like vehicles ground slowly towards them, churning up long streamers of dust. A distant sound of firing, heavy guns, echoed on the morning breeze.

In the same instant, the first of the tanks lurched from its path. The distance was too great for Stone to tell just what had happened. He only knew that the armored titan was veering, jerking, rolling over.

A fraction of a second later it disappeared in a spurting, concussive burst of flame.

Now beyond it, a second vehicle was in trouble. A third.

The fourth exploded like a gigantic exclamation point of fire.

From then on, the battle turned into a rout.

With no survivors.

Sickness twisted at Stone's belly. Fighting it down, he swung back to the pilot. "I won't risk your neck, lieutenant. Land me on the mesa, and be on your way."

WORDLESS, the pilot shifted the whirlybird's controls, setting the 'copter down on a rocky plateau.

"If your CO bawls you out, remind him I had a gun," Stone said. He opened the door; jumped to the ground.

The helicopter was rising again almost before he could turn.

But not for long.

Because suddenly, seemingly out of nowhere, half-a-dozen flying robots swooped down.

Stone never could be sure that the pilot even saw them. They came that fast.

As they passed over the 'copter, the one in the lead dipped slightly. A tentacle speared out, whipped round; stabbed into the blur of spinning rotor blades.

Then it caught, with a jerk so violent that the robot spun from its course, too fast for the eye to follow.

But only for a moment. Then, bobber-like, it came into balance again, the rotor still dangling from the tentacle.

Like a crippled bird, the helicopter plunged earthward...struck with a rending crash...shattered into flames.

Shuddering, Stone crouched motionless in the shadow of a boulder.

Yet, incredibly, the robots gave no sign that they sensed his presence. A moment later they were gone.

Tight-lipped, Stone left his haven and trudged on across the mesa. A mile. Two.

Then, abruptly, the tableland fell away before him. Dropping flat on his belly by the rim, he stared down in grim fascination into the canyon below; for there, surely, lay one of the strangest things the eyes of man had ever seen.

It was a sphere—a shining gigantic metal ball, fully three hundred feet in diameter, if Stone could judge. No lines or ports or crevices marred its gleaming surface. Nowhere about it could he see any sign of life.

Quickly he drew back from the rim, well out of view of the sphere. Then, rising, he strode left, following the mesa's edge till he came to a spot where the eroded lip cut back enough to hide him from the globe-shaped craft.

Slipping and falling, bruising and tearing, he descended to the canyon's floor, then made his way back towards the sphere.

Here, studying it at a lower level from a hidden vantage-point amid the talus, he gained a better, clearer picture.

Three stubby legs gave the globe balance on the uneven bedrock of the canyon floor. A broad, inclined ramp led to a slot-like belly hatch. Of monsters or robots he could see no trace.

74

Stone sucked in air—a long, deep breath. This was the thing he'd sought, the aliens' ship; and now he'd found it.

To what avail?

Somewhere in its maw, by all odds, lay Reva and MacDougal. Yet what could he do about it? How could he, alone and armed only with his Smith & Wesson, hope to invade it or to save them?

But he'd known the odds before he started—and he'd still come. Logic and hazard simply had no bearing.

Surging up, gun in hand, he moved warily forward, hugging the mesa wall.

Now he came abreast the sphere. The ramp to the belly hatch beckoned, smooth and inviting.

Inviting as madness.

A nervous spasm knotted Stone's belly. When it had passed, he stepped out from the wall moved forward, cat-footed, towards the ramp.

Still nothing happened.

Going around the edge of the ramp, he peered up through the open hatch, into the sphere-ship.

THE interior shone with a dim, greenish glow. Overhead loomed a bulwark. He could see nothing more. The stillness was deafening, unbroken save by the whisper of the desert breeze far above.

A new chill shook him.

He might have turned back, then. He almost did.

But in that same moment, as he started to draw away, a voice echoed thinly deep in the globe-craft.

Reva's voice, ragged and strain-straught.

It caught Stone like a magnet. His doubts fell forgotten. Soundlessly, he swung up onto the ramp...crept shadow-silent on into the hatchway.

A corridor yawned, dim in the ghostly green glow. Hardly daring to breathe, Stone sidled along it past doors; littered chambers.

It ended at a tube-like, vertical shaft set off by a guardrail.

The ship's axis, probably.

Stone strained his ears, listening. Again Reva's voice came—louder, this time; vibrating down the shaft.

Swinging out over the guardrail, Stone peered upward.

The shaft was smooth as glass—without handholds or bracing.

He dropped back to the corridor floor.

A closed double door to his left, next to the shaft, tempted him. He stepped towards it.

Like magic, it parted before him, silent as death. A steep ramp curved to the right, following the tube-shaft.

Finger tense on the thirty-eight's trigger, he moved up it, higher and higher.

Each ninety degrees arced brought a new door, a new level. When he approached them, they opened; when they opened he listened.

And each time, Reva's voice sounded closer.

He could hear MacDougal, too, now, on occasion, speaking in rumbles. The very nearness brought sweat oozing. A dozen times he had to switch the gun from one hand to the other to scrub his palms dry of slickness.

Another level. Another. Another.

The level.

Tension drew a band tight over his chest—compressing, constricting. His neck ached. His blood pounded.

Jaws tight, gun-hand rigid, he moved down the passage.

A doorway. An open doorway, flooding out brighter, whiter light.

Back to the wall, Stone edged to it...stared into the room it revealed.

Reva sat on a low, curving divan across from MacDougal. Her pale face showed deep strain-lines; her hands twisted, white-knuckled.

MacDougal's whole body sagged limp and exhausted. The shaggy brows stood out over eyes deep-sunk in dark hollows. His right arm hung in a sling.

Stone swayed for a moment, not daring to think, then slid forward—taut, noiseless.

MacDougal's head twitched. His eyes flicked towards the doorway.

"Quiet—!" Stone shook as he whispered. "For God's sake, be quiet!"

Reva, MacDougal—they both jerked like puppets.

Stone hissed, "This way—quick!"

MacDougal's jowls quivered. His left hand gripped the divan as he heaved up from it.

Eyes distended, breasts rising and falling too fast, Reva followed.

Stone stepped back.

The tentacles folded round him, then.

He triggered his gun by sheer reflex.

The thirty-eight roared—wild, aimless. The bullet rang, bouncing off metal.

The tentacles only drew relentlessly tighter. One slapped at the gun, tore it loose from his fingers.

Another looped round his throat.

It was like a nightmare—a mad repetition of that blood-curdling moment outside Reva's building.

The tentacle drew tighter. Stone's lungs exploded.

The blackness closed in...

CHAPTER EIGHT

THE man beside Stone kept talking, talking:

"They let you get all the way in before they grabbed you, didn't they? They like it like, that—to lead you on, coax you, let you think you're going to win before they kill you. That's how they played it with me. And my wife. Did I tell you about her? They let her run and run, clear across the mesa. All the way down to the highway. Only then a car stopped, so they grabbed her and killed her. They told me about it. They thought it was the best joke ever…"

Stone tried to sit up, to focus on the speaker.

He fell instead, retching.

The man said, "Don't worry. You're not really hurt. It's just those damn tentacles, those snake things they use for arms. They choke you, and tear you, and scare you so you get sick just thinking about 'em. I know. I had it, that night on the mesa—"

"You—"—Stone half-choked—"—you…saw robots?"

"Robots—?" A quavering laugh. "Sure, I saw robots. Robots on the mesa. That's how it all started. Ellen and I—we didn't know it was a government reservation. We were out for some fun. Some fun! Prospecting, believe it or not—prospecting for uranium with a homemade Geiger. Just a fool high-school science teacher and his wife, out on vacation. Only then we got up on the mesa, and I saw the robots. Ellen was scared, but I said, 'Let's get closer.' So they saw us—the squids, here. Caught me. Killed Ellen. Poor Ellen…"

The man's shoulders shook. Then jerked, harder and harder. Anguished sounds came from his throat in dry, racking spasms. "Poor Ellen—"

Stone fought his own stomach; won, lurched up, still panting. Slowly, his vision cleared.

Beside him, the stranger sobbed more wildly. He no longer seemed even aware of Stone's presence. "Why'd they have to leave me, Ellen? Why didn't they kill me, too? That's what I wanted. But no, they had to have someone to go out in the sun. They can't stand the sun, can they, Ellen? Oh—Ellen—!"

His voice rose to a shriek. His face came up into the light—cheeks and chin stubble-matted, eyes wild and staring.

With an effort, Stone reached out and caught one jerking shoulder. Savagely, he slapped the man's face, palm and backhand.

The racking sobs slowed. Wonderingly, the man slumped to the floor, rubbing his cheek. "You—you hit me…" No anger rang in his words—only baffled incredulity, the puzzlement of a hurt child. His eyes stayed wide open, appallingly empty.

Pain under his breastbone, Stone said, "Sorry, friend. You were going to pieces. You've got to get steady or you won't last long, here or elsewhere."

"Last long? Last long?" The other fondled the words. "Who's going to last long, once the squids get their krypton?" A wild giggle. "You know about krypton? Did they tell you?"

Stone felt himself stiffen. "What about krypton?"

"'Must have!'" Again, the man giggled. "Can't run a spaceship without any krypton. Can't fly the robots. Can't even blast a little ole Earth city. 'Krypton! Must have!' They'll get it, too. From that base. It's already surrendered. The people were scared, just like we are. Especially after what happened to the tanks. So the whole base surrendered and started working on that extractor, the krypton extractor. They'll have it finished by tomorrow morning. Then the squids'll get their krypton. And they'll keep their promise too—not hurt anybody, leave right after they get it. They all say so. That'll be the best joke of all—a whole world doing a pratfall right into hell. The squids'll laugh and laugh and laugh, all the way back to Arcturus Four, or Betelgeuse, or wherever it is they come from. Except they can't go back. Not really. They're outlaws, you know, running away from their own species. That's how they happened to get this far from their source of krypton. 'Krypton! Must have!' Can't run a space ship without that vital krypton—"

THE stiffness in Stone had turned to sudden chill. He caught the babbling man's shirtfront; shook him roughly. "Run that through again...the part about the joke, the world doing a prat-fall!"

A vacuous smile. "You really don't know? You don't know about krypton? I thought only fool high-school science teachers didn't know. And Ellen. Poor Ellen—"

"The krypton! What about the krypton?"

"It's a gas, that's all. An inert gas. About two parts to a million of air. It's not worth anything. Nobody wants krypton. Nobody but the squids. Who cares about a little ole catalyst?"

"A catalyst—?"

"Sure. Doesn't do anything itself; just changes the rate of a reaction. Try to light dry phosphorus, what happens? Nothing. Dampen the air a little, it burns like a house afire. Water's the catalyst. Atmosphere's the same way. Mix oxygen and nitrogen and everything else but krypton—it just dissipates, leaks away into space. Shoot in two parts of krypton to a million, it holds together like a sack around ole

Mother Earth. That's why there's no breathable atmosphere on so many planets. No krypton. Do we know that? No. But the squids know it. That's why they're laughing. Why should they waste time blasting us? Soon's they get our krypton, our atmosphere thins away—*poof!* like that—and we all drop dead. The squids don't care; they don't breathe air like we do. It's the best joke they've had since they blew up Vega Seven…"

Stone's legs were suddenly too weak to hold him. His companion's continuing compulsive word-flood echoed unheeded.

The whole world doing a prat-fall into hell.

Stone's flesh crawled. The poor, tortured creature beside him had phrased it too well. It turned a man's mind off, froze his brain…left him clutching in free fall without strength even to shudder.

Yet there was nothing he could do—nothing, nothing. Not here, sealed in this green-glowing, metal walled room with a madman for company.

A madman—? There'd be two of them soon. Two lunatics, giggling and babbling as the atmosphere thinned and, they slowly strangled.

Or would you strangle? Maybe, with the pressure change, your lungs would burst first…

Stone surged to his feet in a spasm of frenzy. Savagely, he hurled himself at the door—beating it, tearing at the crack with his fingers till the nails broke and blood streamed, weird in the green glow.

His companion stared at him, wide-eyed. "You're hurting your hands. Is something the matter?"

"The matter—?" Stone shook with fury, frustration. "No, nothing's the matter. The base has surrendered. The monsters get our krypton. Our air leaks away. The whole planet dies. Everything's fine—fine…"

He broke off, unable to go on.

"Oh…" The other sounded hurt, plaintive. Then: "Well, why don't you stop it? Call the base. Have them blow up the extractor."

"Call—the—base—?" Stone stopped breathing.

"Yes. The machine's in a room right down the hall, here."

Stone choked back his tension…spoke gently, soothingly:

"Our door's locked."

"Oh, that." His companion giggled. "Leave that to me. I'll get us out of here."

Already, he was scrambling to his feet; stripping off his shirt.

"But if you can get out…" Stone groped.

"It takes two." Tearing the ragged shirt into broad strips, the man hummed a fragment of tune. "I thought it all out. If I'd had Ellen with me— I can run the machine, too. I watched them do it. It's very clever. Sets up a force field, distorts radio waves. Using energy derived from krypton, of course. Always krypton. 'Must have!'" He broke off. "I'll need your shirt, too, please. And your jacket. Got to have cloth. Lots of cloth…"

Wordless, Stone turned over his garments.

DEFTLY, the man ripped them into more of the broad strips…tied the strips together in a long, rope-like band perhaps six inches wide. He'd stopped talking now. An occasional mirthless chuckle replaced his giggling.

The job done, he handed Stone one end of the strip. "Now stand here, please. Right beside the door. That's all you need to do. Just stand there, and hold onto the cloth. I'll take care of everything else. Just you wait and see."

He kicked off a shoe; hammered the edge of the sole on the door.

It made a dull, clanging noise. "They don't like this. It'll get our door open. Just you wait—"

Stone waited—sweating, staring numbly.

It was a fine way to end up playing games with a madman.

Only he had no choice.

The next instant, the door burst open. Tentacles vibrating furiously, one of the aliens swept into the room.

The man with Stone stepped back lithely, dodging the creature. The wide, vacant eyes shone bright, now; teeth showed clenched behind the empty smile.

The alien surged towards him.

Again, the man leaped back, the cloth strip coiled loose between his hands.

The alien reached for him.

But instead of retreating, the man darted in close. Deftly, as a matador swirling his cape past a charging bull, he slapped the cloth strip over the monster's scarlet sensor band.

The rope snapped tight in Stone's hands as the alien lurched against it, then tried to draw back.

But the man would not let it. Racing round it, he whipped the fabric strip tight into place, completely covering the creature's narrow scarlet girdle.

Heedless of tentacles, Stone leaped to join him.

The cloth reached three times around the monster's midriff. The alien reeled blindly—groping, uncertain. Its tentacles' movements seemed mostly directed at tearing free the fabric. When a disc caught Stone's shoulder, he jerked it loose with no skin loss.

"Come on!" This from the madman. "Quick! This way! Hurry!"

Stumbling through the doorway, Stone sprinted down the corridor after him.

Now another door loomed, close by the tube-shaft. "Here!"

Stone threw himself at it.

It burst open under his impact. He crashed to the floor of the chamber beyond, barely glimpsing a mass of equipment as he fell.

Equipment—and another alien.

The thing flung itself on Stone, its tentacles twining.

Savagely, he twisted; drove his heels up with all his strength, straight at the monster's sensor band.

The alien rocked back.

Stone leaped up. Then, head low, he charged in, smashing the monster back into the doorway by sheer bull strength and violence.

Another charge—butting; fists slamming.

The alien hit the guardrail encircling the tube-shaft.

Stone glimpsed blurring motion: His fellow-prisoner, diving in low and bear-hugging tentacles. Through his red haze of fury, it came to Stone dimly that the other's last shred of sanity must have departed.

Only then, of a sudden, the man was surging up, jerking.

The knee-leverage tore the alien's lower tentacles loose from the floor. With a heave, the man flipped the creature over the rail.

It plummeted down the tube-shaft.

"Two hundred feet!" Stone's companion cried shrilly. "Listen! It may spatter—!"

NAUSEA writhed in Stone. He caught the other about the waist; dragged him bodily back into the room—up to the equipment.

"Quick! How do I work this?"

"Don't worry. It's easy." The man tugged at a smooth, round shaft of metal. A faint humming sound rose from a flat gridwork. "There. It's on now. Just talk into the grill, there."

Stone had trouble with breathing: "Base! Las Crescentes—"

Behind him, metal rang on metal. He spun round.

An alien stood poised in the doorway—an alien with shreds of cloth still clinging round its middle.

The words he'd planned stuck in his throat.

Only then, as from afar, another voice echoed. The voice of the madman.

"You know—"—it was almost conversational, the way he said it—"—you know, I think I'll go see Ellen…"

He scooped a jagged strip of metal from a bench as he spoke. Traces of froth showed at the corners of his mouth.

Then, before Stone could move, he was lunging, straight at the monster. The metal strip slashed deep into the scarlet sensor band. Fluid spurted.

The alien hurled itself backward.

But like one possessed, the madman pursued it, hacking and gouging. Together, man and monster crashed into the guardrail.

A wild shriek of mad laughter. "Here I come, Ellen—with company!"

Clutching a dozen tentacles, the man hurled himself over the guardrail.

The monster went with him.

Stone clung to the transmitter, half-retching.

Only he couldn't afford to be sick. Not here; not now.

Time was too short for that. Any moment now, there'd be other aliens coming.

Hoarsely, he rasped, "Base! Las Crescentes! This is Carl Stone talking. I'm giving you an order: Destroy that tower! Blast it! Don't wait a minute! If it goes into operation, the whole earth will die…"

CHAPTER NINE

TOGETHER, they stood at last in the free air of the desert—Stone, Reva, MacDougal.

Slowly, half a mile away, the great shining metal ball that was the alien sphere-ship lifted from the gathering shadows of the canyon floor. Soundless as nightfall it rose, drifting higher and higher. The three stub legs retracted.

Then, of a sudden, it had topped the mesa's rim. Faster it climbed, and faster, picking up speed with every passing second.

The blink of an eye later it was gone, up into the dusk and the boundless space that stretched from star to star.

For a long, long moment the silence held. Then MacDougal said quietly, "There aren't any words for what I want to say, Carl. But—the world can never repay you for what you've done."

And Reva: "You saved us. Carl—us, and all the unborn generations that will ever live on Earth."

It was strange, Stone thought. By all the rules, he should feel the same way they did. Happy. Relieved. At peace.

Grateful for the breaks he'd gotten, at least.

Instead, inside, he felt only aching emptiness and pain.

But however he felt, he had to find words. They were expected. The other—the ugly, unfinished job he had yet to do—that could wait.

Shrugging, he said, "The boys at the base are the ones who rate the credit. They worked fast—two minutes flat from the time I passed the word till they shot an anti-tank grenade right into the middle of that damn tower, if our friends the monsters had it right."

"You're over-modest, Carl." MacDougal gestured with his still sling-bound right arm. "You're the one who did the job, and I'm going to see that people know it. The right people."

"Thanks." The word came out faintly caustic, even to Stone's ears.

But maybe that was only the aftermath of strain.

If MacDougal caught it, he ignored it. His craggy face stayed tolerant, relaxed. The hedgerow eyebrows didn't even bristle.

"The big point is, it's over," he reminded. "The aliens and their ship are gone. Our own world's safe."

Reva moved restlessly, drawing her torn dress closer about her, as if touched by a sudden chill. "I hope so. I still don't feel quite as if I were awake. There's so much I don't understand—so many, many things…"

Stone's voice was just above a whisper: "For instance—?"

"You mean—you haven't thought about it? —About why those creatures didn't harm the base, in spite of all their threats? Why they let us go, when it would have been so much easier to kill us?"

Stone didn't answer.

MacDougal said, "I think it's easy enough to understand. The alien's whole technology is based on krypton, and it's in short supply. Destroying the base would have cut down what little reserve they had left, with no return."

"And letting us go—?"

The base director's heavy shoulders shifted. "That's almost a rhetorical question, isn't it, Doctor Adams?" The slightest of edges barbed his words.

Deep in Stone's middle, the pain and emptiness seethed anew.

That was the trouble with unfinished jobs. They kept forcing themselves onto you, when you least wanted to have to think about them.

Only now this particular ugliness was coming out into the open in spite of him. He'd have to face it, grapple with it.

Even if it tore his soul apart.

REVA was staring at MacDougal. "Rhetorical—? I don't understand. What do you mean?"

"Then I'm afraid I'll have to be brutal, Doctor." The base director let out a gusty, sighing breath. "Perhaps you don't realize the nasty role you've played in this whole business. If so, I'm sorry. But the fact remains that in all likelihood Stone and I are alive and free only because of you."

His tone made Reva draw back just a little. Once more, she pulled her torn dress about her, with a movement strangely awkward for one so graceful.

"You'll have to speak more plainly, Mr. MacDougal," she said sharply. "I don't understand you at all."

"Very well, then." MacDougal's massive head came forward, jaw belligerently outthrust, "I'm saying flat-out that you were the aliens' contact. Your mind was the one they took over when they first landed. You were the one who set up the transmitter in your project building and turned the whole base mad. Is that plain enough for you to understand?"

The torn dress bunched under Reva's fingers, an ugly, lumpy wad.

MacDougal again: "I'll carry it even further, Doctor. The aliens don't plan to drop that contact with you. And that's the only reason why the three of us are free."

Even through the gathering dusk, Stone could see the pallor that sprang to Reva's face. Fear widened her eyes. She seemed to grow smaller, older.

It twisted like a knife inside him...made him wonder bleakly how long he could go on.

"Did you think they'd really left for good, Doctor Adams?" The base director's sarcasm rang open, bitter, now. "How far do you estimate they can go—with their krypton reserves already so drained that they didn't even dare to blast our base? To Aldebaran? Antares? Alpha Centauri?" He laughed—curt, scornful. "No, Doctor! They'll be back, somewhere close by, in hours, not light-years. Then, when they get here, they'll contact you. There'll be another transmitter, another base gone mad. And this time, maybe, they'll get their krypton—that is, if Stone and I are fools enough to let you live!"

There it was, out in the open. All of it.

Or almost all.

The blood rang in Stone's ears.

Reva's face was a twisted, distorted thing. Her face seemed to crack. Her lips peeled back. "No, no!" She was half-screaming. "You're wrong! You're wrong—!"

The base director swung his thick, sling-bound right arm—hammering, relentless. "Then why did they let us live? Why—except to keep you free and above suspicion, ready to serve them another day?"

Silence. Echoing eternities of silence.

Then, abruptly, Reva's shoulders slumped. Her chin sank to her chest. She didn't speak.

Slowly, MacDougal straightened. Grim-faced, he looked at Stone. "Well Carl?"

More silence. A sickness, too…gnawing through Stone, body and brain.

Why did it have to be like this? Why couldn't it have ended another way?

MacDougal said, "I'm sorry, Carl. I know how you feel. But this is just too big for us. We can't take chances. The world's at stake. We've got to act now, before the aliens come back."

Stone couldn't speak.

"She can't be allowed to leave this spot alive, Carl. You and I—we'll have to serve as judge and jury. Executioners too. Here. Now."

Stone looked at Reva.

Her eyes were upon him. Grey eyes, imploring. "Carl—!"

MacDougal: "I'm sorry, Carl…"

Tension. Surging billows of tension. Blood pulsing. Heart pounding.

Why couldn't it have ended another way?

Only this was the way it was. These were the cards he had to play.

So he'd play them—

Stone said, "You've figured it right, Mac. All but one point."

"One—? What—?"

"She isn't guilty. You are."

THE base director stood like a graven image. Then his sling hand twitched, just a fraction. That was all.

Stone said, "It all rides on one thing, Mac: You keep talking about the aliens having some sort of mind control over Reva. But it's not true. Violence is the only weapon they know how to use."

MacDougal's lip twisted. "You forget the transmitter."

"The transmitter?" Stone shook his head slowly. "That came second, Mac. Not first. Because somebody had to help the aliens design it—somebody working of his own free will."

"She did it, then. She's the psychiatrist."

"No, Mac. She couldn't have. It took a scientist—a physical scientist, one who knew electronics." A pause, while Stone drew a deep breath. "That's why it has to be you, Mac. You're the man with the know-how. Even if Reva could have done it, you'd have had to pass on it, o.k. the construction; that's part of your base director's job."

"I see."

"You had the motive, too, Mac. And I understand it: When you found The Project was failing, you blew up, clutched at straws. Then the aliens came along and contacted you, somehow. They offered you their own special straw with a hook in it. Probably they promised that if you'd help them get krypton, they'd figure you a new angle on The Project. And you were so afraid of failing, washing up your career that you grabbed at the chance. The hook—you were too eager to see it. After all, nobody on Earth knew that krypton was a catalyst, holding our atmosphere together. How could you guess it?"

"Your logic's good, Carl." MacDougal nodded slowly. "You've done some straight thinking. But if what you say's true, then where does it leave us? I've made a mistake, but what have I done wrong?"

"You still don't see it?"

"I'm afraid not."

"Then I'll tell you." Stone sighed, just a little. "To you, Mac, your career's too important. If you think it's in danger, everything else has to get out of the way. Like here, now. You'd have had us kill Reva—to give you a goat, and keep me from talking. There'd be no black marks on your record. Maybe you even picked up a few tricks from the monsters that would make The Project go."

"So—?" The base director spoke very gently.

"So it won't wash, Mac. I'm security. It's my job to see straight, and to push out people whose careers mean more than duty."

"We've been friends a long time, Carl—"

It was Stone's turn to nod. "That's what makes it so hard, Mac. Maybe if the aliens come back, you'd have an H-bomb all waiting. Maybe. But maybe not, too. Maybe you'd bite on another hook—one that would really catch, give the monsters their chance to laugh and laugh and laugh, all the way back to Arcturus Four—" Stone broke off abruptly. "No, Mac. We can't take that chance. I'm sorry."

"I'm sorry, too, Carl." The heavy shoulders shifted. "Because—it means I have to kill you, as well as Doctor Adams."

Stone frowned. "That might take some doing."

"I doubt it." Of a sudden there was ice in the base director's voice—ice, and granite. His sling-suspended hand moved sharply. "You see, I've got a gun here, Carl. My arm isn't really hurt, but the sling seemed like good cover." He laughed, harsh and short. "Any last words—?"

A numbness came to Stone's middle.

How far was he from MacDougal? Three steps? Four? Too far.

He looked over at Reva.

SHE stood as before, still clutching her torn dress. The bulkiness of the fabric lumped in her twisting fingers was like a deformity growing out of her side. Strain had stolen her face's last traces of beauty. Her blonde hair hung limp and straggly.

Stone didn't care. Of a sudden he could think only of all the words unspoken between them; of the long years that should have been theirs, the feelings crumbling down into ashes.

Inside him, the emptiness swirled to a churning vortex. "Reva—!" he whispered. "Reva…"

"Time's up!" MacDougal said. His sling-hand flickered out.

Stone lunged at him.

Only it was too far, too far. He knew it even as he charged. MacDougal's bullet would cut him down in mid-stride.

And then Reva would die. He sobbed a curse that came out as a prayer.

MacDougal's gun leveled, rock steady.

Stone braced for the slug.

Only then—suddenly; incredibly—another gun roared. A gun off to one side, from where Reva stood.

MacDougal jerked round, firing wildly.

With every ounce of his weight. Stone crashed his fist against the heavy, jutting jaw.

The base director's head snapped back. Like a pole-axed ox, he toppled to the ground and lay there motionless.

Stone picked up the gun and stuck it into his belt. "Reva—"

She came to him, then—running, arms out, the torn dress forgotten.

For a long moment, Stone held her. "You...saved my life."

"With your own gun." Of a sudden, she was shaking. "It landed beside me, back there on the sphere-ship. I hid it under my dress—for myself. I didn't want to die with tentacles around me..."

Her voice broke. She buried her face on Stone's shoulder. He held her close.

"We're not going to die," he said gently. "Neither of us. Not now. We've got too much to live for." Her face came up slowly. "To live for!" she echoed.

Never, Stone thought, had he seen her so beautiful.

Together, then, hand in hand, they walked out across the desert towards the distant highway.

THE END

If you've enjoyed this book, you will not want to miss these terrific titles…

ARMCHAIR SCI-FI & HORROR DOUBLE NOVELS, $12.95 each

D-31   **A HOAX IN TIME** by Keith Laumer
          INSIDE EARTH by Poul Anderson

D-32   **TERROR STATION** by Dwight V. Swain
          THE WEAPON FROM ETERNITY by Dwight V. Swain

D-33   **THE SHIP FROM INFINITY** by Edmond Hamilton
          TAKEOFF by C. M. Kornbluth

D-34   **THE METAL DOOM** by David H. Keller
          TWELVE TIMES ZERO by Howard Browne

D-35   **HUNTERS OUT OF SPACE** by Joseph Kelleam
          INVASION FROM THE DEEP by Paul W. Fairman,

D-36   **THE BEES OF DEATH** by Robert Moore Williams
          A PLAGUE OF PYTHONS by Frederick Pohl

D-37   **THE LORDS OF QUARMALL** by Fritz Leiber and Harry Fischer
          BEACON TO ELSEWHERE by James H. Schmitz

D-38   **BEYOND PLUTO** by John S. Campbell
          ARTERY OF FIRE by Thomas N. Scortia

D-39   **SPECIAL DELIVERY** by Kris Neville
          NO TIME FOR TOFFEE by Charles F. Meyers

D-40   **JUNGLE IN THE SKY** by Milton Lesser
          RECALLED TO LIFE by Robert Silverberg

ARMCHAIR SCIENCE FICTION CLASSICS, $12.95 each

C-10   **MARS IS MY DESTINATION**
          by Frank Belknap Long

C-11   **SPACE PLAGUE**
          by George O. Smith

C-12   **SO SHALL YE REAP**
          by Rog Phillips

ARMCHAIR SCI-FI & HORROR GEMS SERIES, $12.95 each

G-3   **SCIENCE FICTION GEMS, Vol. Two**
          James Blish and others

G-4   **HORROR GEMS, Vol. Two**
          Joseph Payne Brennan and others

THE HIGH COST OF FREEDOM...

Once again, the Federation was ruled by madmen, twisted by their greed and lust for power. These unruly brutes sought the "ultimate weapon" to quash the raider planets for good and claim the known universe as their prize.

But Jarl Corvett was a daring freeborn raider who thought of those who'd lived, and those who'd died—and whether they lived or died for good or evil.
He thought of freedom…

Here is another great tale from Dwight V. Swain, a master story-teller not only in the field of science fiction, but in the mystery, western, and action adventure genres as well, with dozens of novels and short stories to his credit.

CAST OF CHARACTERS

JARL CORVETT
Free-born raider, his was ready to die for the cause of the raider worlds, to whom his loyalty knew no bounds.

UNGO
Battle scarred, but loyal. He'd come on a fool's mad mission— and now was prepared to fight to the death.

KTAR WASSRECK
He sought answers that lay on another world, but finding them meant being labeled a traitor.

SAIS
One could only guess what thoughts had been in her mind when she tried to kill the man she claimed to love…

YLANA REY GUNDRE
She had learned a terrible secret, and trusting a raider pirate in her plight was no easy choice—to say the least!

BOR LEGAT
A Basilisk of Mercury, murderous and merciless, yet loyal in his own twisted way to the raider cause.

THE WEAPON
FROM ETERNITY

By
DWIGHT V. SWAIN

ARMCHAIR FICTION
PO Box 4369, Medford, Oregon 97504

*For more information about Armchair Books and products, visit our
website at…*

www.armchairfiction.com

Or email us at…

armchairfiction@yahoo.com

CHAPTER ONE

JARL Corvett selected the group—himself, Ungo, and five crewmen.

They left their great ship on the far side of Vesta; came down with the night in a fast raider carrier.

A hollow offered shelter. Like dust settling, they landed. Abandoning the craft, they pressed on towards their target. The hills fell behind. The final cordon was bypassed.

Then, at last, bleakly, they stared down at the sprawling building that had been Wassreck's workshop.

But lights beat on the white walls. Guards paced the parapets. The commissioner's own carrier thrust up in the courtyard.

Frowning, Jarl Corvett crouched deep in the shadows. Tension crawled his spine like a leather-footed *palau*. His own black thoughts pressed relentlessly in upon him: *Is this where it ends, warrior? Is this the place, here under the Federation's dazzling Forspark lights, on a tiny astroidal speck that men call Vesta?*

Beside him, the darkness rustled. Scales brushed his arm. One-armed Jovian Ungo's hoarse whisper echoed over-loud in his ear: "Give it up, Jarl! Wassreck's gone, and they're ready. It's hopeless!"

"It was hopeless before," Jarl Corvett said tightly. "It was hopeless at Horla. But Wassreck came for me."

The Jovian's scaly hand gripped his shoulder in the darkness. "I know, Jarl. You're loyal. But this time—"

"Could you face Sais without trying? Could you tell her you'd left him?"

Ungo grunted, half-sullen. "Will it help if you're killed, too? Will it make her feel better?" He cursed in his own tongue. "Me, I still like living. I'm not ready to die yet."

Jarl threw off the Jovian's arm. His words slashed, raw and savage, in spite of his efforts: "You can leave if you want to: I ask no man to risk his neck against his will!"

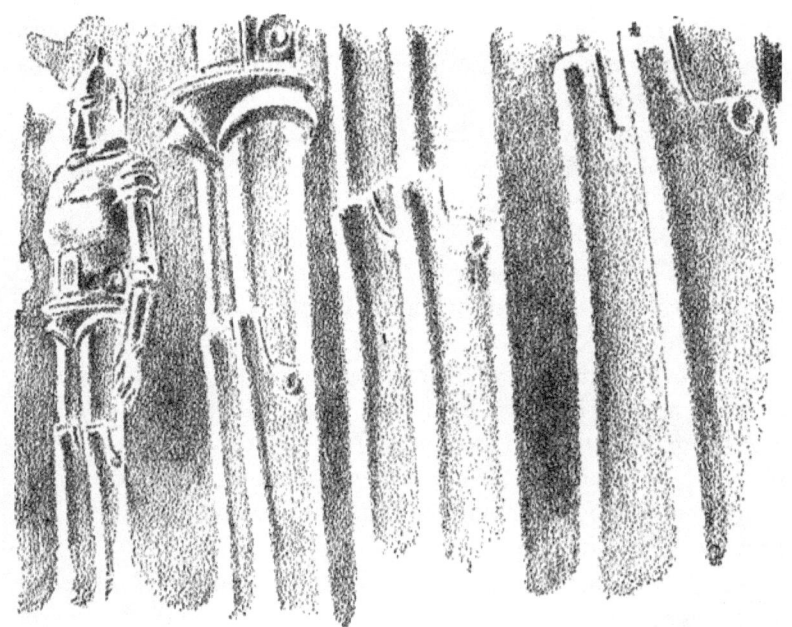

THE WEAPON FROM ETERNITY

By

Dwight V. Swain

Legends spoke of a weapon too dreadful to use hidden somewhere among the stars—a weapon that was its own master — choosing its victims!

Dimly, against the sky, he could see Ungo's head sink down between the great, horny shoulders. "Don't gall me, you *chitza!* I go where you go! I always will!"

Jarl clenched his fists. He thought: *Yes, Ungo will always go where you go, Jarl Corvett. He proved that when he left one arm on Pluto for you. That's what's wrong with loyalty. It traps you, tears you two ways. Because whichever road you take, good men, good friends, must die.*

And Sais would be waiting.

HE cursed aloud and crawled forward, away from big Ungo, digging in knees and elbows with savage force, taking out his fury on the rocky ground.

Ahead, just outside the blazing lake of light around the building, the air-vent loomed. Wriggling to it, he jerked out his knife and pried at the grilled lid's seal.

But then, once again, Ungo was beside him. "Here, let me at it, Jarl!" Heedless of danger, the Jovian surged to full height. His talon fingers splayed through the grill. The broad back, the mighty shoulders, strained and heaved.

There was a thin *spang!* of metal parting. The lid tore free.

Jarl gripped his comrade's arm. "Ungo..."

"Forget it, Jarl. I understand. Our job is down below."

A tightness came to Jarl Corvett's throat. Wordless, he swung his legs over the edge of the vent, lowered himself to full arm's length, and let go.

It was a six-foot drop into blackness so ebon that it made the outer night almost seem bright. Twisting, he crawled a few feet along the horizontal conduit that ran from shaft to building.

Ungo's gruntings drifted down as he wedged his great body through the hole. Then, with a thud, the Jovian, too, had landed. The other five followed, one by one.

"This way!" Jarl whispered. "The tube leads straight to the blower room."

Ghost-silent, they crept through the murk for what seemed miles. Fine dust rose about them in a choking haze, and there was an acrid stink of tanaline and *jeol.* Tiny *bulaks* chattered their fright, scampering from the raiders' path. The suction of the Banx unit at the tunnel's other end tugged at hair and tunics in a gusty, whistling gale.

Then, feeling ahead, Jarl touched a screen. He halted; half-turned. "We've made it. We're inside." Twisting, he ran his hand over the tube's sidewall till he found the cleaning hatch. His searching fingers touched the bolt. He worked it round.

The hatch swung open on creaking hinges. Knife in hand, Jarl slid out into the blower room, with its looming bulk of Banx unit transmuters and converters and compressors.

A dim rectangle on the right marked the ramp to the floor above. Cat-footed, flat to the wall, Jarl moved up the incline, the raiders at his heels.

A faint scuff of sound whispered in the stillness. Ahead, out of a cross-corridor, a Martian *fala* in the blue tunic of a Federation guard moved into view.

Jarl froze, not daring to breathe.

The guard crossed the ramp, not pausing, and went on down the corridor out of sight. The shuffle of his steps faded and died.

Jarl slid forward again till he reached the passage, then halted. Taut-nerved, he waited, listening.

Voices came dimly. Jarl lowered himself to the floor. Ever so cautiously, he peered around the corner.

FAR down the hall, the guard stood chatting with one of his fellows. A moment later, breaking off, he turned and started back towards the ramp again.

Jarl drew back. Rising, he wiped the sweat from the palm of his knife hand, then crouched waiting.

The sound of the *fala's* footsteps drifted to him, closer and closer.

Jarl sucked in air.

The scuffing echoed through the silence. The guard stepped out onto the ramp.

Jarl leaped forward—catching the *fala's* chin from behind, jerking back the ugly head, slashing at the throat.

The guard's cry died in bubbling purple blood. He wrenched spasmodically, hands and feet threshing; then went limp.

Jarl dragged him backward—out of the corridor, down the ramp. Breathing hard, he lowered the sagging corpse to the floor.

Ungo touched his arm, gestured questioningly.

Jarl whispered: "The living quarters are upstairs. They'll have her there."

The Jovian nodded, not speaking.

Again Jarl dropped flat and wormed forward, searching the corridor.

No one was in sight.

Surging to his feet, he swung right down the hall to the next ramp, his crewmen behind him. Swift, silent, he raced to the second floor.

There were no guards here—only echoing stillness and blank closed doors.

The first room was empty. In the second snored a sleeping *dau* captain from the Federation fleet.

Big Ungo whispered hoarsely, "This one's locked!"

It was the door at the end...the door to the room that had once been Sais'.

Jarl pressed against it. Sheathing his knife, he brought out a light-gun and pressing its muzzle against the lock, squeezed the trigger.

The silent beam blazed forth. The lock's bolt fused and fell away.

The raiders pushed into the room.

A girl lay in the bed, asleep. Quick, tight-lipped, Jarl crossed to her side.

She was it vision of slim blonde loveliness, this woman. A golden vision from a far-off world. As he looked at her, the thought flickered through Jarl Corvett's mind: *She's almost as beautiful as Sais.*

Dark Sais, *Ktar* Wassreck's daughter...

Yet even while the girl slept, a deeper, darker mood seemed to shadow her loveliness, as if she held some brooding secret locked within her. Or perhaps it was only that a strain of clouded alien blood ran in her veins, from her mother—blood of Titan, or Io or Venus.

"Is this her, Jarl?" big Ungo whispered. "Is she Ylana? Time's running short..."

Jarl shook off his mood. "Yes. She's the one, the commissioner's daughter." He caught the girl's shoulder and jerked at it roughly, one hand to her mouth, in case she should scream.

SHE came awake with a start, grey eyes flaring wide in sudden panic. Her whole body convulsed as she saw the raiders.

Jarl threw himself on her, bearing her down. Fiercely, he whispered, "Quiet, if you wish to live!"

Her struggles ceased. Lips pale, breasts heaving, she lay stiff and unyielding.

He said: "Relax, woman! We're not going to hurt you."

Her lips moved on his palm. He raised his hand a fraction.

"Who are you?" Her voice shook. "What do you want here?"

"They call me Jarl Corvett."

The girl clutched her throat. "Jarl Corvett, the raider? The ally of Wassreck—?"

Jarl smiled at her thinly. "Ally, friend, comrade, brother. That's why I've come here. I needed a hostage."

"A hostage—?"

"For Wassreck. He's a prisoner. You'll buy his freedom."

The grey eyes distended. The girl breathed fast and shallow, ripe lips half-parted. "You madman—!" she whispered.

Jarl Corvett laughed harshly, and there was ice and fire in it. "Some say so. But Wassreck saved me at Horla. Tonight I've come here to pay back what I owe him."

"Jarl!" Ungo broke in, raw-voiced and urgent. "Quick! Hurry! They will find that dead guard any minute!"

"Yes." Jarl raised up. He spoke again to the girl—bleak, cold, rock-steady: "You're coming, Ylana. As to how—you do the choosing. But even if we have to tie you and gag you and carry you, you're coming!"

The girl's grey eyes probed his. Color came to her lips; they no longer trembled. "You mean—you really believe you can

105

storm in here and take me? That your handful of raiders can fight through the cordon—?"

"Freemen have done more."

"Freemen—?" Ylana's laugh was tight, bitter. "What do you and your outlaws know about freedom? To you, it means nothing but freedom to murder, to plunder!"

Her words stung like gas-hail slashing down upon Pluto. Jarl felt his breath quicken. "Who are you, to talk of the outlaw worlds and their plunder?" he lashed back at her fiercely. "What of your father's own fleet; your thrice-cursed Federation?"

The girl blazed. "The Federation brings order!"

"And what is your order but another name for plunder—the great planets' power to take what they choose from the lesser?" Jarl choked on his anger. "To you, I'm a pirate, because men like me sweep the void in our own raider ships to keep our people from starving. What else can we do, living on these barren rocks in the Belt, charred fragments of worlds that should never have been colonized? But your father—with no right on his side but the Federation fleet's might, he's named high commissioner—sent out to tear even our bleak asteroids from us by conquest—"

"Jarl—!" burst out Ungo.

"I'm coming!" Jarl towered over Ylana. "Get ready!"

THE girl sat up in her bed. Her fists gripped the covers tightly. "I warn you, Jarl Corvett: You'll curse the day that you took me—"

"Because of your father?" Jarl laughed, short and curt. "I'll still chance it."

"No." The girl's grey eyes seethed, dark and dangerous. "Because of me, Ylana *rey* Gundre! Because I'll see you and your men die in torment, a thousand times worse than the flame-death at Horla—"

"I'll chance that, too." Jarl jerked back the covers.

Wordless, disdainful, the girl tossed her head. The golden hair rippled. Rising, she took a gown from a chair and pulled it about her slim, perfect figure.

"That's better." Jarl turned to Ungo. "We'll go down through the workshop. There's less chance there to trap us."

In hair-triggered silence, they moved back through the hallway, the girl boxed among them. A different ramp yawned. The door at its foot let them into the workshop, the place of the robots.

Wassreck's robots.

A name to conjure with, *Ktar* Wassreck. Master of robots. Master of raiders. The brain of a genius in a pain-shriveled body. A mind that had fathomed the key to the star-stones; courage to strike even through Oyo's flame-death, staking his soul for Jarl Corvett at Horla.

And here were his robots—towering metal monsters, set shoulder to shoulder. He dreamed of them, lived for them. More even than dark Sais, they were his children.

Children of a nightmare, Jarl thought as he led the way past them. Bleakly, he wondered why Wassreck had made them— what dark, twisted drive had spurred their creation.

They came to a door. Jarl faced his raiders. "The hallway's outside. The third ramp to the left leads down to the blowers."

He turned to the girl, the commissioner's slim daughter. "Stay with me, Ylana. And forget about running or screaming."

She moved closer, not speaking. The grey eyes were unfathomable.

He stepped into the passage, the girl close behind him. The crewmen followed.

Then, as they came abreast the second ramp, he heard voices—a harsh, angry crackle that rose louder each second.

Jarl stopped in his tracks and spun round to the crewmen. "Quick! Up the ramp—!"

Gripping Ylana's wrist, he half dragged her with him.

Barely in time, they crowded into the entry. Down the hall, by the blowers, someone cursed loudly. More footsteps pounded. Metal banged metal.

Big Ungo burst out, "It's that guard, Jarl. They've found him—!" He clutched at his blaster—head down, geared for battle.

Now new steps hurried towards them, from the way they had come.

Jarl whipped out his light-gun. "We're not done! The commissioner's carrier is out in the courtyard. We'll blast our way to it!"

"Which way—?"

"Back up this ramp! We'll drop from a window!"

THEY sped up the incline to the second level, then down the corridor. But before they could reach a room that opened on the inner court, tumult broke out on this upper floor also. Guards shouted. There was a beat of feet; the clamor of men rushing towards them.

Jarl leaped for a doorway. "In here—on the double!"

His men crowded past him. Shoving Ylana before him, Jarl followed. Inside, he half-closed the door.

Like statues, they waited. The hurrying guard squad came closer.

Jarl gripped Ylana tight, her slim body hard against him. He cupped his hand over her mouth. The golden hair brushed his cheek. He could feel her heart pounding.

The first of the blue-uniformed Federation fighters ran past the half-open door.

Jarl poised his light-gun.

In the same instant, lance-sharp pain stabbed through the hand he held over Ylana's mouth.

He jerked back by instinct—and knew of a sudden even as he did it that the girl had bitten him.

But his flinching left Ylana's mouth clear for an instant. She screamed, shrill and piercing.

Jarl cursed. He tried to throw her aside.

But she clutched his belt, clinging. Snatching his razor-edged knife from its sheath, she slashed at him.

He rocked backward, off balance.

The girl twisted. He glimpsed her face—teeth bared; features strain-straut. Backhanded, she lashed at his temple with the knife-haft, her full strength behind it.

It struck home as the first guards burst through the doorway...

CHAPTER TWO

TWIN blue-and-silver Federation banners marked the place of the high commissioner of all the asteroids.

His table stood at the far end of the vast room that had been *Ktar* Wassreck's workshop. Other tables radiated out in a great arc from it—tables crowded with officers of the Federation fleet. Heavy-thewed Uranian *daus* sat side by side with slim reptilian *Pervods*. *Transmi* of Venus, all ear-stalks and sucking tubes, faced rubbery, flat-featured Europans. Creatures of half a hundred divergent races, hybrids and mutants, they gathered here from all the far-flung planets of the Federation. Their rising voices clashed in strange cacophony through the tinkle of cutlery and crystal, thrown back in a din of ringing echoes from the giant metal robots that still lined the walls.

Straightening in spite of the weight of his shackles, shrugging off the hands of the guards who flanked him, Jarl Corvett met the seething hostility of their glances with stiff-necked defiance. But underneath, questions nagged him: *Why am I here? Who ordered me brought to this banquet?*

But here he stood. That was what counted. Boldly, he surveyed the room...stared unflinching across at the commissioner.

A handsome man, Commissioner *rey* Gundre. Heavy-bodied and aging, in these later days. But still personable, still a figure to catch the eye, even slack-faced and slouched in his seat as now.

He was a man of Earth, plainly, with all the strengths and weaknesses and surging conflicts that went with that heritage. The sunburst insignia of his rank stood out against the deep blue of his impeccably tailored uniform. The white blaze that accented the darkness of his hair only made him the more striking.

His aide sat at his left hand, Ylana at his right.

Ylana the golden, daughter of the high commissioner himself.

And Jarl Corvett's nemesis.

Even looking at her here, Jarl could feel the muscles at the hinges of his jaws draw tight.

Tonight she sat slim and graceful at the banquet table in a scarlet stylon gown. Her blonde hair swept up in a soft golden nimbus like that of Tal Neeni, sea goddess of Callisto. The red lips were smiling, the grey eyes asparkle.

Yet even when she laughed, some dark inner mood seemed to shadow her beauty, even as it had last night while she lay asleep.

That shadow... Was it alien blood, or a secret? Again Jarl caught himself wondering. He thought: *I should hate her!* And in the same moment: *Even Sais is no lovelier...*

Cursing himself for a fool and a weakling, he tore his eyes from her and studied the aide.

He was *Malya,* this officer; *Malya* and warrior. His dark rough-hewn face stayed emotionless, immobile. But the black Malya eyes ranged ceaselessly—bleak and, watchful, never still. Ruthlessness was in them, and recklessness...a spirit that seemed to mock Jarl Corvett and deny the blue Federation tunic that the dark aide wore.

BITTERLY, Jarl looked down at his shackles. He thought of the *Malyas* among his own crewmen; the wild, freeborn raiders.

How long would it be before they, too, wore the blue of the Federation?

Or, before they died…

Now the commissioner stirred. Chin sunk on chest, he mumbled something to his rock-faced lieutenant.

The lean aide nodded briefly. Twisting in his seat, he pounded on the banquet table—first with his fist; then the butt of his heavy Talistan ray gun.

The sound rose even above the tumult and raucous voices, echoing and re-echoing through the great room that till short days before had been Wassreck's clandestine robotics laboratory.

Slowly, the noise and voices died away. Chairs scraped. Heads turned. Eyes of *Fantay* and of *fala*, Mercurian and Martian, *Chonya*, Thorian, *Pervod*, searched out the table where the aide and the high commissioner sat.

Not quite steadily, then, the commissioner rose, a brimming *kabat* goblet in his hand. His eyes had the glassy shine of bright new mirrors, and his tunic was rumpled, twisted awry.

Swaying a little, the commissioner slapped loose-fingered at the blouse, as if to brush away the wrinkles. *Kabat* slopped from the goblet and spilled over his hand. Blinking, he looked down at the spreading green stain. A foolish grin flickered fleetingly on his face.

Ylana leaned towards him; spoke sharply.

The commissioner's head twitched. He straightened, and his shoulders snapped back to a too stiff 'attention'. Jerkily, he raised his glass.

"A toast to our host, officers!" he cried in a drink-thickened voice. "A toast to *Ktar* Wassreck—may he rot in hell!"

Leaden silence came down on the room like a curtain. Furtive glances flicked out to the towering robots, shoulder to shoulder, that lined the walls.

It made Jarl Corvett smile a little, the way the officers hung back. Did some recall H'sana? Were others on Pallas? Free or captive, *Ktar* Wassreck still put cold fear in them!

Ktar Wassreck: Outlaw, scientist, scholar. Wassreck at Horla—gnome head tilted, eyes burning, laughing in the face of death. Wassreck…and Sais…

Spasmodically, Jarl's fists clenched. His bruised head throbbed dully.

"To our host!" the commissioner cried again, lurching forward. "To Wassreck—"

The spell broke. The officers surged to their feet. Their shouts rang through the clamor: "To Wassreck—"

"—May he rot in hell!"

They drank it down.

Fury swirled up in Jarl Corvett, hot and all consuming.

Swaying, face flushed, the commissioner clutched a decanter. He spilled more *kabat* into his goblet. "Now—one for Corvett! A toast to Jarl Corvett—"

HE broke off as Ylana tugged at his tunic. Lines of angry tension slashed the smooth loveliness of her face. Her lips moved, wrapping round curt syllables.

Her father laughed drunkenly.

He turned towards the doorway where guards and raider stood, and his hand swept up in a clumsy broadside gesture. "Drag him out!" he shouted. "Flush the *chitza* out of his hole!"

The two Mercurians who flanked Jarl closed in. One clutched his arm.

Jarl's fury seethed higher. In spite of his shackles, he jerked free of the Mercurian's taloned hand. He felt cold arrogance ring in his voice: "No one drags Jarl Corvett! I'll walk alone!"

For the fraction of a second the guards stood hesitant, lobed eyes clouded beneath their nictitating lids.

Jarl swung his arms back sharply.

The chains of his shackles whispered, link on link, like a flexing metal knout.

The Mercurians' eyes fell. Contemptuous, ignoring them, Jarl turned away. Head high, back unbending, he strode towards the table of the high commissioner.

The Earthman smirked at him, still swaying.

Recklessness sang a death-song in Jarl Corvett's veins.

"Hail, coward!" he cried fiercely, and swept the crowd with a scathing glance. "Is this the best your Federation fleet can offer—scum so low that they draw their sport from taunting prisoners? *Huroks* so green with fear that you must bring me here in bonds?"

An angry babble rose from the tables, and the commissioner's *kabat*-heavy lids drooped lower. But his lips twisted in the mirthless semblance of a smile.

"Do you rate yourself so high that you think I'd waste time on you, *starbo?*" He laughed, deep in his throat. "No, brigand! You're here against my will!"

"Against your will—?"

"Yes. You're here to face another—one whom even I cannot deny, after what you've done."

Wordless, narrow-eyed, Jarl studied him for a moment. "Then who—?"

"Who would it be?" This time the commissioner's laugh was sour and savage. "Can you not guess, *yanat?*" And then: "My daughter, Ylana."

"Your daughter—!"Jarl pivoted to Ylana.

"Yes!" The girl came to her feet as he turned, grey eyes blazing. Her words burst forth in a scalding flood. "Did you think I spoke empty words when I swore last night that you'd live to curse the day you tried to seize me? Did you take my promise for a hollow threat—?"

She broke off; swept round the table, a furious vision in gold and scarlet. Her hand flicked up in a tight, peremptory gesture. "Atak! Seize him—!"

The commissioner's rock-faced *Malya* aide closed in on Jarl, moving round behind him.

Ylana raised a shaking fist. "On your knees, *stabat!*"

A numb incredulousness crept through Jarl Corvett. But he stood the straighter. "I kneel for no man—nor for woman!"

A savage kick in the back of the knees caught him from behind in the same instant. His legs buckled. He spilled forward, asprawl on the floor.

"A whip—!" cried Ylana, face white with passion. "A whip for this raider dog they call Jarl Corvett!"

One of the Mercurian guards sprang forward, jerking off his heavy, *stanal*-buckled belt. "Here, *Shi* Ylana! The plate will cut deep!"

The girl snatched it from him. Her face contorted.

"No, Ylana—!" It was her father, the *kabat*-haze fading from his eyes. "Would you drag yourself down to the level of this *chitza*, here before officers of the fleet—?"

The girl turned on him as a *quirst* turns on its pursuers. "Who talks of dragging down, and of the fleet?" she lashed fiercely. "Do you dare to speak—you, with your plots and schemes, your secret meetings—?"

The high commissioner flushed to the hair. "Ylana! Silence!"

"Was it you this *starbo* and his scum dragged out of bed last night? Was it you who screamed and called the guard when they sought to flee in your own carrier?"

Her father's jaws went stiff and set. His clenched fists bore down upon the table. But he broke before Ylana's eyes; said nothing more.

The girl turned her back on him. Furiously, she challenged Jarl: "You were brave enough last night, when you dealt only with a helpless woman! But how is your courage now, bold raider? How does force taste, when another hand holds the lash?"

Her shoulders twisted. Gripping the Mercurian's belt by the tongue, she slashed out with the heavy *stanal* clasp.

Jarl rocked back. The buckle sang past his face, so close he could feel its breath.

But now, again, the *Malya's* foot caught him from behind. It knocked him forward on his shackled hands, off balance.

Before he could recover, the belt whipped down again. The buckle tore at his cheek. He rocked with pain.

"Is it different, this time, raider?" Ylana shrieked. "Are you ready to sing another song?"

Tight-jawed, stiff-backed, Jarl met her gaze. He did not speak.

The girl's red lips peeled back. "I asked you a question, dog!" she cried. "I want an answer!"

She slashed out with the belt again. The buckle seared his jaw and neck.

"Answer me!"

Wordless, Jarl swayed.

The buckle ripped at his forehead. Blood gushed down into his eyes.

"Answer me—!"

Jarl lurched forward, clutching for her. But she darted back, out of his reach. The stylon gown rustled. The buckle tore a path along his scalp. The room blurred and swam before his eyes. Desperately, he tried to cover his face with his shackled hands. But the tangled chains were too short. He could only double forward, face to the floor.

THE buckle struck behind his right ear with stunning force, a fiery knife stabbing through a red haze of pain.

"Wait, Ylana—!" It was Atak the *Malya's* voice, drifting dimly to Jarl as from afar. "Those blows to the head—he cannot last—"

"Then drag him up! Tear off his tunic! Bear his back, so that I can see the red blood run!"

Hands clawed at Jarl's clothes.

He felt his tunic rip away. The aide dragged him up; twisted him about.

"Hold him there, Atak! Hold him tight!" came Ylana's cry.

The buckle seared Jarl's back—once, twice, a dozen times.

"Speak, *starbo*! Beg for mercy as you made me beg—!"

Jarl fought against showing pain as the girl brought the belt down on his back.

Jarl cursed her with a raw, pain-surging hate; cursed her with all the black epithets of a raider and the warrior worlds.

"Still stubborn, *chitza*—?" Wild hysteria was in Ylana's voice. The buckle bit in again.

Atak's hoarse whisper rasped in his ear: "You fool, give up! The woman's mad! Even a raider should know that there's a time to crawl!"

Jarl clenched his teeth.

The girl cried, "You see, Atak? He loves the lash—!"

She struck again.

The commissioner's voice slashed harshly, the fog of drink long gone:

"Ylana! You'll kill him—!"

"You—!" The girl's contempt was a writhing, burning thing. "Where were you last night, you *kabat*-soaked sot? You, with your talk of duty, your fat-puffed pomp—"

Her father's voice went clipped and tight. "Enough, woman! Raider or not, this man's my prisoner. Tomorrow I'll ship him on to the Venus headquarters. He'll die in the *slan*-chambers there; not by your hand." The room echoed with the flat slap of his palm cracking down on the banquet table. "Atak! Get his tunic! Send him to his cell."

"Yes, Excellency…" The *Malya* let go Jarl Corvett's arms.

Blinking the blood from his eyes, the raider stood swaying. Still numb, still not quite believing, he stared at golden Ylana, in her scarlet stylon gown.

Now, her hair hung down, no longer nimbus. Her lips were pale, and her breasts rose and fell too fast. Madness gleamed in her dark-circled eyes.

She snatched the tunic from Atak. "Here! Let me…" Whirling, she ran to Jarl and thrust the wadded garment into his shackled hands. "Brave raider—!"

She spat full in his face.

The *Malya* aide caught her arm and jerked her back. "If you were not *rey* Gundre's daughter—" He cursed under his breath. "Get out! You disgrace us!"

Gripping Jarl's arm, he led him from the hall. "I cannot expect your pardon, Jarl Corvett. It would be too much to ask from any raider, any man. But in their day, my ancestors roved the void…"

His voice trailed off. Turning to the guards, he said, "Take him to his cell. I'll see that one of the fleet *ktars* comes on down."

WEAK, tottering, Jarl let them lead him back to the old, thick-walled wing they had given over to the prisoners. He had not even the strength to curse when the guard, a Martian *fala* with all his race's fiendish love of cruelty, tripped him skillfully, so that he sprawled on his face as he crossed the threshold to the room that was his cell.

The door clanged shut on the Martian's ghoulish laugh. Sick with pain, Jarl dragged himself up and crawled to the bunk. Belly-down, he sagged onto the springless frame.

How long he lay there he never knew. It was all he could do to breathe, to be. The room about him was a reeling, distorted world of mists and feverish dreams.

Then, at last, that, too, passed. Wearily, he pulled himself upright and shook out his wadded tunic.

Metal clanged on the floor.

Jarl stiffened in spite of his wounds. Swiftly, he bent and felt beneath the bunk.

His hand touched metal. It was a knife...a keen, long-bladed telonium fighting *skrii.*

For a long, long moment he sat in silence, gripping its heavy haft. Then, in the darkness, he slowly smiled.

A *Malya* was still a *Malya*, whether he wore the Federation's uniform or not.

Tomorrow they'd ship him to the Venus headquarters, the *slan*-chambers, death.

But this was tonight, the darkest hour, and he had a knife, and the high commissioner's carrier still stood in the court outside...

CHAPTER THREE

THE fleet-bell was tolling the nineteenth hour before the *ktar* came down.

Lying in the darkness, waiting for him, Jarl battled in stubborn silence against the pain. He found himself giving heed to a thousand little things—the roughness of the pollard—

weave against his lacerated cheek…a prowling *peffok's* distant cry. Faint, pervasive scents of doloid dust, of must and *jeol*, pressed in upon him. He savored the raw taste of blood in his mouth…the saltiness of sweat when he ran his tongue along his lips. Once, dimly, he caught the harsh rasp of Ungo's voice, drifting to him from some other room.

Ungo of Jupiter, Big Ungo the loyal. He'd come here, protesting, on a fool's mad mission. And now…

A flood of black doubt welled up in Jarl Corvett—doubt of himself, his world, his cause. Would his dreams end here, in this dreary cell? Would morning find him lancing out through space on his way to Venus and the *slan*-chambers?

And…would Wassreck die?

Writhing, fists clenched, he tried to drive the vision of the burning eyes, the pain-racked body, from his brain.

But the image, the dark thoughts, would not go away.

Because Wassreck was on Venus already. Wassreck had no hope, save in him, Jarl Corvett…

An incoherent, protestful sound rose in his throat. Spasmodically, he gripped the bunk's chill metal frame; twisted as if to rend it, tear it apart.

The effort made his tortured muscles shriek with pain. His ears rang. The room rocked wildly. He gasped and sagged forward, plunging down through green-and-purple depths of icy fire into a bottomless, slowly eddying pool.

Then the pool resolved. Of a sudden he was looking into Sais' dark eyes. She was smiling at him, a tender smile, and her fingers were cool against his cheek, her soft lips welcoming his.

But a misty barrier rose between them, a barrier of heart and mind that seared like a white-hot iron: *How can I face her? What can I say, if her father dies?*

He cried aloud, a hoarse, choked cry, and Sais' face vanished. Once more, the room closed in upon him. Again he lay straining on the bunk—tasting the blood, drinking in the stink of doloid dust and *jeol*.

Sais, and Wassreck. Wassreck, and Sais.

He wondered if he'd ever see either of them again.

Somewhere outside, a vague new stir of movement broke the stillness.

Jarl stiffened. For a moment he grasped the knife. Then, relaxing, after a moment's hesitation, he slid the sleek blade out of sight beneath his leg.

The sounds drew nearer; finally paused outside his cell. A blur of muffled, grumbling words seeped through the door. The bolt clicked back.

It was the *ktar*, a dead-white four-armed *kroy* of Ganymede. Flicking on the light, adjusting the vocodor translator, the creature brushed smoothly into the room. Behind him, the *fala* guard lounged idly back against the jamb; thumbs hooked in his belt.

JARL shifted, then lay still again, not speaking. He was thankful to Atak—thankful the *Malya* had sent a Ganymedan *ktar*. Few were more talented or highly skilled or kind.

The *ktar* crossed to him and set down the globe that held the impedimenta of the healing craft. "How is it, raider?"

Jarl grunted and lifted his shoulders a fraction in a shrug.

The *ktar* probed the cuts that gashed Jarl's back with deft, sure, pseudopodal fingers. "Nasty. That thrice-cursed *stanal* buckle bit deep," Swiftly, he cleaned the wounds and applied the healing gel.

Jarl winced and clenched his teeth.

"Up, now," the *ktar* commanded. "Let me at your face."

Stiffly, Jarl twisted. Keeping the precious knife covered with his buttocks, he swung his legs to the floor and sat up.

The *ktar* worked on in silence for a time. Then, at last, he straightened. "That does it." He laughed—wry, almost bitter. "By the time you get to Venus, you'll be in the best shape to die."

Picking up the globe, he pivoted and, with the peculiar floating motion of his kind, moved towards the door.

Jarl gripped the haft of the telonium *skrii*. Tension came alive in him, hot and quivering. Rising from the bunk, he followed the *kroy*, holding the knife out of sight behind him. "I thank you, *ktar*..." He dared say no more for fear his voice might betray him.

The Ganymedan muttered something incoherent and passed out into the hall. The *fala* guard, in turn, planted a many-jointed arm appendage hard against Jarl's chest and roughly shoved him back. His mottled throat-sac quivered. "No farther, *chitza!*"

Wordless, Jarl swayed. He made a show of cringing.

The *fala* laughed harshly. His bulging eyes flicked to the hall outside. Turning, he gripped the door handle and started to pull the portal shut.

Jarl leaped at him like a pouncing *zanth,* stabbing for the throat-sac with the keen-edged *skrii* blade.

The point bit in, even as the Martian tried to throw up a warding arm. What might have been a shout came out as a rush of blood and bubbling air.

The *fala* tottered, coughing out his life. Down the corridor, the Ganymedan whirled.

Jarl snatched the ray gun from the toppling guard's holster. His voice rasped, low-keyed and tense: "Don't make me kill you, *ktar!* I want only freedom, not your life!"

The *kroy's* eyes flicked down to the leveled gun. He stopped short—stiff, silent.

"Back here!" Jarl clipped. "Back in my cell..."

Wordless, dead white face a chalky mask, the *kroy* slithered past him.

"Take him with you!" Jarl gestured to the fallen *fala* guard.

The *ktar* bent. His pseudopods locked onto the dead Martian's shoulders. He dragged the corpse out of the corridor, into the cell.

Jarl swept up the wave-pencil key from where it had fallen as the *fala* died. Tight-drawn as a Uranian *tal*-string, gun still lined on the Ganymedan's neuro-plexus, he jerked the cell door shut and slid the wave-pencil into its slot beside the lock.

THE bolt clicked home. A fierce excitement flared within Jarl. Heart pounding, heedless of the fatigue and pain that racked him, he spun about and ran, half-reeling, down the hall.

He wondered how much time he had.

Or if he had any.

Wassreck and Sais. He gripped the ray gun tighter.

The first three doors he passed stood open.

The fourth was closed and locked.

Jarl slid the wave-pencil into the slot.

The bolt snapped back. Shoving open the door, he strained his eyes, searching the darkness of the room.

A thick, familiar voice snarled sleepily from a bunk.

"Ungo—!"

The great, horny shoulders heaved up. The misshapen head lurched into view. "Jarl—!" It was a half gasp, half sob. "Jarl, I thought they'd done for you—that you'd gone under—!"

Jarl reeled against the Jovian, clutching the mighty arm. "Quiet! They'll be after us any second!"

He could feel Ungo's muscles swell. "Let them—!"

Jarl laughed in spite of his tension, his pain. "Not yet, Ungo. Not till the job is done!" He pivoted. "Come on!"

The Jovian's head sank down between the bulging shoulders. His eyes gleamed. "The tube again—the way we came—?"

Jarl paused at the door. "No." He peered up and down the corridor.

"Then what—?"

"The commissioner's carrier. It's still in the court outside. We'll grab it as soon as I get back." Jarl started forward.

Ungo caught his wrist. "Jarl…"

"What—?"

"There may be something you don't know…"

Jarl came around sharply. "Speak up! Time's short!" Once more, the tension was climbing in him.

Ungo fumbled: "The guards—they talked a little. They say the reason *rey* Gundre went all-out on this raid was for a weapon, more than Wassreck."

Jarl felt the cords along his neck draw tighter. "A weapon—?"

"Some new thing Wassreck worked out. A beam that focuses energy drawn from cosmic dust." The Jovian's voice sank lower. His head thrust forward. "Jarl, they claim it'll blast a ship right out of space, at almost any range. They've got it geared and mounted now."

Jarl braced himself against the door. It dawned on him that his palm was slick with sweat against the ray gun's butt. The little things came back to him—the tastes, the smells, the sounds. Again he peered up and down the empty hall.

A weapon that focused the power that lay in cosmic dust—? Even to talk of it was sheer madness!

Yet Wassreck had made madness come to life so many times...

Involuntarily, Jarl Corvett shivered.

"If it's true, they'll blast us down before we even get the carrier to our ship," said Ungo. He scrubbed his scaly hand along his hip. "We wouldn't have a chance..."

JARL bit down hard. With savage effort, he forced himself to think; to shake off the bleak despair that kept rising in him, ever higher. "What chance could we have if we went back through the tube, the air-vent?"

"We could maybe hide"

"On Vesta—?" Jarl laughed aloud. "They'd find us as easily as in our cells!" He broke off. The laughter went out of him, replaced by an urgency even more feverish than that which had gone before. "No, Ungo! It means we've got to run! We'd have to even if we could find a place to hide!"

"But why, Jarl—?" The big Jovian scowled and fumbled.

"A weapon like that, and you ask why?" Jarl cursed in harsh, bitter syllables. "What about the others—the outlaw worlds?

What will it mean when the Federation fleet sweeps down on H'sana?—on Ceresta?"

It was Ungo's turn to curse. Jarl shoved the wave-pencil into his hand. "Here! Break out the men! And hurry!"

"But you—"

Jarl laughed. Of a sudden, once again, recklessness was boiling in him. "We came here on a mission!"

"Not the woman—!"

"She'll still make *rey* Gundre hold his fire! She'll still buy Wassreck free!"

Ungo twisted. His bulk loomed rock-rigid, bigger than ever. "You can't, Jarl! I won't let you! You are sick—crazy—"

The fire of recklessness in Jarl glowed brighter. "Tell me that tomorrow, Ungo!" he clipped through clenched teeth. "You may convince me—after the commissioner's ordered his men to shoot us down with that hell-cat aboard!"

Ungo's breath came faster. "Then let me go, Jarl! Let me get her—!"

Jarl brought the ray gun up, stone-steady. "We may both die on Vesta, Ungo. That's enough for me to have resting on my conscience."

"But Jarl—"

"I'll shoot if I have to, Ungo."

Their eyes locked, and for a long moment they stood statue-like, unmoving. Then, half-sullenly, the Jovian stepped aside. "I'll be waiting, Jarl. Whatever happens, I'll be waiting."

Jarl did not answer. Of a sudden there were no words for him to say to Ungo. Ray gun in hand, he ran down the hall, picking his way through the maze of ramps and corridors.

He thought: *It would have been better if Wassreck had let me die on Horla.*

Then, at last, he reached Ylana's room. It came to him as a shock when there was no guard.

Silently, he opened the door; stepped swiftly in, gun up and ready.

The bed, the room, were empty.

IN a sort of frenzy, he ran through the rest of the suite; jerked open the neutron-bath and closets.

But the girl was gone.

He spun about, for a wild moment ready to race on through the rambling building, searching further.

But that was madness, and in his heart he knew it. Not even a clue as to Ylana's whereabouts had been left behind. He might hunt for hours to no avail.

And time was running short...the seconds ticking by.

Jarl sagged back numbly. The fire went out of him. A dinning echo drummed within his brain: *I've failed...I've failed...I've failed...*

Wassreck had gone through Horla's holocaust for nothing. Sais would weep and turn away.

As for Ceresta.

But there was still Ungo to think of...Ungo, and the five dauntless, swaggering raider crewmen who'd come here with him. He owed it to them at least to try to get away.

Leaden-footed, he stumbled back through the maze of halls and ramps again.

Then he was back in the corridor of the cells. Ungo lumbered up beside him, eyes alight with a lust for battle. "Jarl! We knocked us off a guard station—!"

The five crewmen crowded around grinning wolfishly, displaying weapons.

Jarl said dully, "Ungo, she was gone."

The Jovian shrugged his massive shoulders. "It goes that way sometimes." And then: "We can't wait, Jarl. The far sky's getting grey already."

"All right."

"We've found a gate to the court..."

"Let's go, then." Woodenly, Jarl walked with them to the heavy door and peered through a crevice into the courtyard.

The personal carrier of *rey* Gundre, high commissioner of all the asteroids, rose stark and sleek, a shining silver lance against the darkness of the sky. Blue-uniformed Federation guards patrolled in pairs or stood their posts around it, weapons dully gleaming.

The sight of the ship, the fighters, somehow lifted Jarl. Of a sudden he knew that now, of all times, he needed a foe that he could see and strike.

He clipped curt orders: "We'll come out fast and trust to shock to get us through. The first man aboard grabs the controls. The last racks shut the hatch. Blast as soon as the bell rings!"

The raiders drew close, weapons ready. Jarl cut through the bolt on the door.

"Now?" whispered Ungo.

"Now."

UNGO'S bulk struck the gate with a splintering crash. The raiders charged for the ship like ravening *zanths* that race to reach their prey.

Knife ready, ray gun ablaze, Jarl Corvett leaped forward in his crewmen's van.

Guards spun about. Desperately, the nearest tried to form to meet the rush.

Jarl drove the knife deep into a *Pervod's* breast; blasted a *dau* back with his ray gun's full charge. The fierce joy of conflict leaped in him. As from afar, he heard the shouts of his men as they lunged into the fray.

The guard's ranks wavered.

But now those from beyond the carrier were rushing to their aid. Steel dashed on steel. A great bulbous-bodied Thorian hurtled down on Jarl. Its tentacles wrapped round him, crushing him.

Savagely, he slashed at the leathery body; blasted with the ray gun, straight into the repulsive face.

The Thorian's tentacles fell away. Jarl glimpsed Big Ungo, smashed down a *dau* with a blow of his one mighty arm. There was a smell of blood and burnt flesh; wild screams of rage and fear and anguish.

"To the ship—!" Jarl shouted.

He hacked his way up the blood-slippery ramp; clutched Ungo's belt and half-dragged the Jovian aboard.

The last of the raiders scrambled in behind them. The hatch clanged shut. The ready bell leaped to jangling life.

There was a sudden roar of auxiliary gravicomps. The gyro-indicators jiggled and swayed in their mountings. Men lurched awkwardly, caught momentarily off balance in the crushing force of too-fast acceleration.

Then stability returned. The carrier speared upward, out from Vesta, into the spark-spangled, glittering murk of the boundless astroidal night.

Jarl turned, seeking out the crewmen, and a sudden sickness gripped him. There were only three now: three and Big Ungo.

But the dead were dead, and they had gone as raiders go. Bleakly, he made his way to the viziscreen and turned it on. Spinning the dials, he drew a cross on the specific black emptiness where his ship had been scheduled to pick them up. His fingers shook a little, and his earlier, darker mood came back to nag him. *We're overdue, a day behind already. What if they've given us up and gone? What if a fleet patrol has flushed them out?*

Grimly, he calculated the carrier's chances of making Ceres on her own…such slim, slim chances…

Only then, as he manipulated the dials, a great, shark-like bulk loomed on the viziscreen. At his elbow Ungo thrust out a quivering talon and cried, "It's her, Jarl! The *Ghost!* She's still waiting!"

Stiff-fingered, Jarl adjusted the focus. The familiar outlines of the raider ship sharpened. Silent, space-drive off, she drifted shadow-like through the asteroids like some strange, cylindrical metal world.

JARL let out his breath, all at once acutely conscious of the strain that frayed at him. He was suddenly tottering weak, his belly sick and twisting.

Still beside him, Ungo studied him with worried eyes. "Look, Jarl: You're done. Lay down before you fall down."

Jarl braced his arm against the cabinet of the viziscreen. "How can I rest?" he mumbled, and knew himself that he was mumbling. "Even if we make it, what happens to the raider fleet—and to Ceresta? This new weapon…"

"Can you help more if you're dead?" the Jovian badgered. "Will things be better if you fall over?" He gripped Jarl's arm. "Come on! I'm putting you to bed, whether you want to go or not!"

Numbly, Jarl let himself be led into the commissioner's own tiny private cabin. Wordless, he sagged onto the bunk.

Ungo backed out again and closed the door.

Flat on his back in the pulsing stillness, Jarl closed his eyes.

But sleep would not come. His brain was a screen, alive with a vivid, ever-shifting kaleidoscope of form and color. Again and again, his mind flicked back to Sais and Wassreck…to the raider fleet, the wild rovers and fighting men he knew so well…to Ceresta's teeming streets, and the cold, bleak beauty of the hills and plains of Pallas.

And to Ylana.

Shifting, he opened his eyes and stared up at the dully-gleaming ceiling.

Where had the girl gone? Why had she not been in her room?

Above all, what strange lust had led her to flay him as she had, before the highest officers of her father's fleet?

Jarl frowned and rubbed his aching forehead. The girl's willingness to bring down upon herself the shame of beating a shackled prisoner was a hard thing to explain.

Could it be that she indeed had alien blood—a strain from some sadistic barbarian breed? Narrow-eyed, he tried to recall her face more clearly…the shadow that hung over her slim blonde loveliness. Or—he frowned again—perhaps that shadow truly hid a secret—the secret of a twisted mind set in beauty's body, irrevocably warping over into madness.

He moved to a more comfortable position, still staring up at the blank inscrutability of the metal ceiling. A play of light and shadow caught his eye. Idly, he followed its shiftings—first slow, then suddenly abrupt, then slow again.

Little by little, an uneasiness crept over him. New tension began to crawl in his midriff.

He loosened his belt and pulled the wrinkles from his tunic; moved from side to side.

But the uneasiness grew. He could not make it go away.

Biting his lip, he lay back, still searching for the cause.

Overhead, the shadows on the ceiling slowly began to shift again.

It came to him, then: He was lying motionless, allegedly alone in this cramped room—*yet the shadows were moving!*

There could be only one answer: Someone else shared these quarters with him.

THE hair on the back of his neck crawled. Grimly, he wondered what the odds on his life would be if it turned out that some *Pervod* guard had been trapped here when the carrier took off.

Twisting in the bed, he let his hand fall across the haft of his knife.

The shadows overhead flexed a fraction.

Ever so slowly, ever so carefully, he turned his head, looking sidewise down at the floor.

A heel was drawing out of sight beneath the bunk.

Jarl gripped the knife. Silently, he twisted still further, till he was in position to strike.

Only then did he speak—coldly, with all the menace he could muster: "Come out—or I'll kill you!"

The whisper of a quick-drawn breath broke through the stillness, then died again in utter silence.

Jarl poised; drew back his knife.

"All right, then, curse you——!"

Clothing rustled. A voice choked, "Wait, Jarl Corvett——! I'm coming…"

A strangely familiar voice…

Again there was the rustling. A head moved into view from beneath the bunk, already turning…a woman's head, crowned with a nimbus of golden hair.

It was Ylana.

CHAPTER FOUR

A DRAGGING eternity of silence echoed in the tiny cabin. Jarl's knife-hand fell. He groped for words that would not come.

Coolly, the girl slid out from under the bunk and supple, graceful, arose to her feet. Ignoring Jarl, she straightened the sleekly styled blue Federation tunic that accented rather than concealed the smooth curves of her slim young body. When she looked up, her grey eyes were mocking, half-disdainful. "What, raider? Have you never seen a woman, that you must stare so at me?"

"You——? A woman?" Jarl spat. "Your own sex would disown you! You're more mad *ban* than human!" He clenched his fist. "By H'sana's virgins, I should kill you!"

Ylana tossed her head—uncringing, defiant. The golden hair rippled. "Is that your raider's way, then? To kill the one who gives you life?"

"Who gives me life——?" Jarl cursed. He touched his lacerated face. "You've given me scars only!"

"Is your beauty such that wounds will mar it?" The girl's lips twisted scornfully. "I thought you'd find my *skrii* worth a few cuts, a little pain, if it would buy you back your freedom."

"The *skrii*——? The knife?" Jarl choked. "You mean—it was you who gave it, not the *Malya*——?"

"Who else?" she shrugged, and her contempt bit like the telonium blade's own razor edge. "Did you think I'd shame myself, beating a prisoner before my father's men, without reason?"

Jarl rocked. "But why——?"

Once more, Ylana's slim shoulders lifted. She smoothed her hair, with elaborate deliberation. "You were too closely guarded for me to reach you in your cell. But it came to me that if I made a show of hate, I could trick my father into bringing you to the great hall so I could confront you before all, at the banquet. The beating—it was the only way I could devise to pass the *skrii* on to you."

Jarl studied her. But her eyes were clear, her smooth face guileless. The shadow of a smile played about her mouth.

He frowned and gestured helplessly. "Does not even a woman need some reason…?"

"I had a reason," she said, and of a sudden she was no longer smiling. "I had so great a reason…"

Abruptly, half-turning, she broke off. Her eyes left Jarl's, and he saw that her hands had tightened to white-knuckled fists. Her breasts rose and fell too fast beneath the tunic.

He waited, not speaking.

Still looking away, her voice the barest whisper, she said, "I learned the truth at last, Jarl Corvett."

"The truth——?"

"About freedom, and the Federation as a partnership of plunder. About my father, and that renegade *chitza* Wassreck." Her voice broke. Her eyes came back; met Jarl's, "Raider, how can I tell you? Wassreck has betrayed you!"

"Betrayed me——?" Jarl went rigid. In two quick steps he was beside her—gripping her chin; staring down into her eyes. "Not Wassreck——!"

"Yes. Wassreck!" Her words came tumbling forth in a rush, raw and defiant. "He was not captured, Jarl Corvett! He surrendered!"

"You lie!"

"No! Of his own free will, he sent a secret message to my father! He had a new weapon, he said—a projector that would break your raiders' power forever. He offered to give it to the Federation, if in exchange they'd lift the brand of outlaw from him and award him a post of proper honor."

NEW fury gripped Jarl Corvett. "You lie!" he lashed again. "You lie in your teeth, you she-*quirst!* This is some sneaking scheme, a filthy trick to match the one you played back there in the banquet hall—"

"No, no..." The girl's voice choked with pain. Tears spilled down her cheeks. "My jaw—you'll break it—"

Jarl let go her chin.

White patches from his gripping fingers marked her face. For an instant, shame flooded through him. Yet, somehow, in the tension of the moment, it only added to his fury. Savagely, he turned away and paced the cabin. "Curse you, Ylana!"

She looked away. The grey eyes were dull, her face deep-shadowed. "I know, Jarl Corvett. You still hate me. You wonder why I should do this thing—give you my *skrii*, tell you all I've told, hide here on my father's carrier so that you would take me with you..." Her voice broke. The tears coursed faster. "All my life, my father's talked of duty. But now, with this new weapon in his grasp, he would keep it secret till he can sweep the asteroids clean for the wealth that's waiting to be seized. He talks of perquisites of office, claims it as his due for his years of service..."

Chill, narrow-eyed, Jarl weighed her words. "So, now, you'd turn against him?"

She hid her face. Her voice came muffled. "It was more than I could stand, Jarl Corvett—that you should die for loyalty, while my father loots the Belt, and Wassreck basks in honor. Now,"—she raised her head, red lips aquiver—"now, at least, I've warned you. You can flee somewhere—perhaps to the dark worlds beyond Pluto..."

"Perhaps."

"Perhaps—? What else is there for you to do?"

Tight-jawed, Jarl slapped his hands against his hips. "I can still go on to the outlaw worlds. My ship can still ramp at Ceresta."

"Ceresta—?" The eager light faded from her face. She drew back, staring. "But why, Jarl Corvett? Don't you understand what I've just told you? The raider worlds are doomed!"

"So you claim," Jarl nodded. "But Wassreck proved himself to me at Horla. Do you think I'd forsake him now, on your word only?" Grimly, again, he paced the tiny cabin. "No, golden Ylana! You—you're still *rey* Gundre's daughter!"

Her hand came to her throat. "You mean—?"

Rock-faced, he towered over her, fighting down all impulses to gentleness, to mercy. "I mean that whether you tell the truth or not, your father's still the high commissioner. How can I trust you?"

He could see the pulse beat in her temple. "Then…it means nothing to you that I hid aboard the carrier, here, to warn you? I pledged my life—"

He nodded curtly. "Yes. You pledged your life. And now it's forfeit!" Turning on his heel, he strode to the door and flung it open. "Ungo!"

The Jovian turned from the viziscreen. "What, Jarl?"

"Come here! We've got our hostage!"

"Our hostage—?" Big Ungo lumbered to the cabin's door, then stopped short, gaping. "Jarl—! The woman—!"

"Yes, the woman! Ylana, the commissioner's own daughter!" Even as he said it, there was a sickness in Jarl Corvett. But he put false triumph into his voice to cover the things he felt. "She came of her own free will, old comrade, with a fool's wild tale that Wassreck had betrayed us!"

THE girl stood rigid. Her mouth, her throat, were working. Then furiously, she stumbled forward and ran to him. Her fists beat a drum-roll against his chest. "You *chitza*—!" Sobbing, she broke off; turned to face Ungo and the staring crewmen. "A fool's tale, he calls it! He'd go on to Ceresta!" She choked. "Must all of us die for this one madman? I tell you, your sainted Wassreck has surrendered and given the Federation his newest, most deadly weapon! I came to warn you, so that you could flee to outer space—"

Jarl caught her arm. Sharply, he twisted. "Enough, you she-*quirst!* Even if you believe you tell the truth, you're more the fool to think so!"

Wincing, doubled with pain, she twisted. "What do you mean?"

Jarl laughed, and the sound came out less mirth than anguish. Did you forget that Wassreck's own daughter, Sais, is at Ceresta? Would he cut loose your father's Federation fleet, arm his deadliest foe with a new weapon, knowing that Sais and the raiders would die together?"

The girl's face paled. "No—! No, it can't be—"

"It can't be, but it is. Sais came to me there, to beg me to try to save her father!"

Ylana swayed. Her lovely face was a mirror of shock. Helpless, grey-eyes tear brimming, she twisted in mute appeal to the other raiders.

Ungo said: "It's true, woman. I was there with him."

"But it can't be…" The words came out almost a whimper.

Across the room, the viziscreen's communicator bell rang shrilly.

Jarl let the girl's arm fall. Muscles stiff, belly tight with tension, he strode to the screen and spun the dials swiftly to the cross shown on the communicator unit.

A room took form upon the screen, a bleak, bare, metal room where blue-uniformed Federation crewmen moved to and fro.

Ungo clipped: "The screen-room—! The screen-room of Gundre's own fleet flagship, down on Vesta!"

Mute, Jarl Corvett nodded; focused.

NOW a new figure appeared before the screen...the iron-backed, handsome figure of High Commissioner *rey* Gundre. Deep lines etched his lean face. His hair was mussed, his tunic-collar open. But he stood erect, and his eyes were cold as Pluto's ice-things.

His voice came, harsh and savage: "You *starbos!* If you've laid one finger on my daughter, I swear by every god from here to Arcturus that you'll die by inches!"

A spark of quick admiration touched Jarl Corvett; and with it came flooding a feeling that was almost pity.

But he held his face cold, and twisted his lips in a mocking, mirthless smile. "Brave talk, Commissioner!" And then: "You can have her back, you know...in exchange for *Ktar* Wassreck!"

rey Gundre's mouth twisted. "You *chitza!* You know he's gone!"

"Then get him back."

"From the *slan*-chambers, the Venus headquarters?" *rey* Gundre cursed.

"From hell, if need be!" Jarl took a quick half-step forward; stood with hands on hips, feet wide apart, in fierce, cold-eyed defiance. He let his voice ring: "The choice is yours, Commissioner! How much do you love her? Take your pick now! It's her, or *Ktar* Wassreck!"

The older man brought up a fist that shook with fury. His face worked in a twitching spasm. "I'll blast you, Corvett! By the gods, I'll blast you!"

"Blast, then," Jarl shrugged. "Blast, and be damned! But re-member—your daughter's with us!"

Things happened to the other's face, then...things that were not good to see. The cheeks sagged, and the mouth went limp, and the eyes' fire dulled to coals of pain. Of a sudden *rey* Gundre was no longer the high commissioner, but only a shriveled husk of a man all at once grown old beyond his years.

He swayed, then turned, as if he had forgotten Jarl and the raiders. "Atak, what can I do—?" It was a plea, a supplication.

His *Malya* aide moved into view beside him on the screen. The dark, rough-hewn face had the set of granite. "Corvett…"

Jarl forgot his pity. Sudden needles of tension pricked at his neck. "Yes."

"Tell me, raider—have you heard of *Ktar* Wassreck's new projector?"

"Yes."

"And that we've already set it up—that at this moment it's geared for action?"

Woodenly, Jarl nodded.

The *Malya*'s eyes grew black as the void. "Then know another thing, Jarl Corvett! Know that we've plotted your course as you ranged off from Vesta."

Chill tendrils brushed Jarl's spine. But he held his face blank, without emotion. "And so—?"

"So you, too, have a choice to make, raider—the choice between coming back, or trying to cross the void in a short-flight carrier."

JARL shrugged and forced the thin vestige of a smile. "A good threat, *Malya*. It might break me—if I believed it."

"But you do not?"

"No projector has the range to reach my ship from Vesta."

"More power lies in cosmic dust than you can dream of, raider." Atak's eyes were bleak, his dark face set in a mask of menace. "You've made your choice, Corvett! Now set your cross for your own ship—and live with the decision!"

The viziscreen went blank.

"Jarl…" whispered Big Ungo. "Quick, Jarl, get a cross on the ship!"

The crewmen's voices were muttered echoes.

With an effort, Jarl kept his movements casual. Wordless, he spun the dials.

The *Ghost's* looming bulk took form, drifting through the emptiness of space.

In the stillness, Atak's voice blared through the audio unit. "Are you ready, raider? Are you watching?"

Jarl cursed him.

The *Malya* laughed harshly. "I press a button…"

Numb, stiff with tension, Jarl stared at the screen, hardly conscious of the crewmen crowding round him.

For a long moment, nothing happened.

Then, before his very eyes, the *Ghost* began to glow.

It came slowly, at first—the faintest touch of pale phosphorescence.

But with every heartbeat, it shone brighter. In seconds the hull was weirdly agleam as with some strange, penetrating light.

Then the ship rocked wildly. He could see the plates begin to buckle.

"No—!" screamed a crewman. "No! My brother—!"

Wallowing, the *Ghost* flamed bright as a *thes*-wood torch. Proton cannon streamed blazing, aimless death. The hull began to cave, then burst asunder. Like an *eidel*-bomb exploding, it tore apart in great, flaring sections that blasted out through space, beyond the viziscreen's frame edges.

Slowly, the weird light faded; died. The blackness of the void closed in.

Like men paralyzed, the raiders stared unspeaking into the awful emptiness where short moments before the *Ghost* had drifted.

It came to Jarl Corvett that he was trembling. Numb-fingered, he reached out and snapped off the viziscreen.

The sound of the switch triggered loose the tension. At his elbow, Ylana burst into hysterical, wildly triumphant laughter. "You see—? Will you believe me now, when I tell you what fate awaits you?"

Pivoting, Jarl slapped her across the mouth with all his might.

She crashed to the floor against the carrier's farthest wall; lay there in a crumpled, moaning heap.

The crewmen fell back a step, all eyes on Jarl. He could not read their stony faces.

"Jarl…" Ungo's voice was shaking. "Jarl, you saw it—!"

The others' words were sullen echoes.

JARL moved away from them a fraction, till his back was against the viziscreen. He let his hand hang close to his ray gun.

He said: "We're wasting time. Even in this carrier, we still can make Ceresta."

They stared at him, all of them—Ungo, Ylana, the three hard-eyed crewmen. Then, suddenly, a *Chonya* blurted, "You're mad, Jarl! What chance would we have against that projector?"

"You can forget the projector." Jarl jerked his head in the direction of Ylana. "As long as she's aboard, they won't dare use it."

"But across the void…" The raiders exchanged fearful glances.

"Would you rather die on Venus?"

Big Ungo shifted. "But Ceresta, Jarl—it's too far to go. There are other places nearer, safer."

"And the raider fleet—?" In spite of himself, Jarl's voice was bitter.

"The fleet—?"

"How long do you think the Federation will wait to strike, now that they've got this new projector?" Jarl laughed, harsh and curt. "By now, the armorers will be fitting them into every ship. Tomorrow they'll be blasting down on Ceres."

He could see new fear come alive in the others' eyes. It put iron in him.

He lashed out: "Are your own necks all that you can think of? Does it mean nothing to you that good friends will die and, with them, all freedom?—That the outlaw worlds at last will be forced to bow their necks to the yoke of the Federation?"

The others' eyes fell. The raiders looked away and shifted.

Jarl said: "That's one of the reasons why we're going to Ceresta. With *rey* Gundre's daughter there, the Federation fleet will hold off striking."

Big Ungo looked up, still half-sullen. "You said that was one reason. What others are there?"

A knot drew tight in Jarl Corvett's belly. "We came to Vesta to save *Ktar* Wassreck. Now they claim he has betrayed us."

"But what—?"

"Sais is at Ceresta." The knot drew tighter. "If it's true, if Wassreck has gone over, then we'll need her for a hostage."

Again the silence echoed.

Then, suddenly, the *Chonya* crewman cried, "To hell with that! You don't give a *filan* for Ceresta!" His voice went raw with angry passion. "We know what you want! It's Sais you're after—not as a hostage, but a woman!"

Face contorted, he clawed for his blaster.

Jarl whipped up his ray gun—twisting, firing.

The *Chonya* crashed back, dead. Hate seethed in Jarl Corvett, a boiling, red-hazed murder-fury. He shook in a spasm of unbridled passion.

"You *chitzas!*" he shouted. "I'll kill you all—even you, Ungo—"

The great Jovian's face twitched.

But there was no fear in it. Bleakly, he lumbered forward, towering. His deep voice rasped: "Kill ahead, Jarl. Any time you want to." His massive shoulders seemed to draw together. "I'm with you now, Jarl. I've always been. But I'll speak my mind when I think I need to—to you, or the devil!"

Jarl's tide of fury ebbed and died. The ray gun dropped to his side, and of a sudden he was shaking. "Ungo…"

"I know, Jarl. It doesn't matter."

Ungo's taloned hand was like a steadying pillar. "Go ahead. Give your orders."

Numb, sick, Jarl Corvett slowly straightened, and breathed deep.

He said, "Our course is still Ceresta!"

CHAPTER FIVE

CERESTA: Port Royal of the void; sprawling, anarchical capitol city of the outlaw worlds.

Here were burrows of Rhea's spider men, and *Pervod* cones, and *Fantay* spires. Hive-like Mercurian domes rose amid the flat-roofed dwellings of the *llorin*. Throbbing *Transmi* drums beat out their savage rhythm, echoing over voices that spoke in Pluto's clacking accents and the reptilian sibilance's of creatures from the ammonia-and-methyl swamplands of Saturn and the Rings. There was the acrid smell of Rogek gas and rocket fuel—and the stink of the bulbous, grub-like *Mah'ham* that fed on their own dead. Here a rover could dine on t's'krai of Callisto, or haggle over the price of one of Neptune's fire-jewels…or have his brains beaten out with a genuine Torod mace.

For this was a warrior's city, haven of the wild, blood-lusting raiders who made the asteroid belt their home. Fighting men from half-a-hundred satellites and planetoids and planets, they gathered here by their own choice, drawn together in one vast cutthroat brotherhood of booty. Old names, old fames, were left unmentioned. The hulls of the battered ships that ramped in the vastness of the sprawling port bore no Federation registration symbols.

Now, in the shadowy dusk that characterized this strange, warped world of Ceres, the carrier of High Commissioner *rey* Gundre came limping down.

Jarl Corvett brought the craft in himself.

He waited till the shadows verged on darkness, enough to hide the carrier's insignia; then picked a spot far off from the tower, out where the port bordered on the old native quarter, and let the ship drop down her gravicomps dead like another, blacker shadow.

The carrier rocked in to a silent landing. Rising from the control seat, he strode to the hatch.

But Big Ungo was already there before him—blaster on hip, massive shoulders straining at the fabric of an appropriated Federation tunic. "Jarl, you can't go alone..."

Jarl Corvett smiled thinly. "I've got to, Ungo."

"But there may be trouble..." The Jovian brought up his one hand in an angry gesture.

"I know. That's why you can't go...I need you here on board more than I do with me." Jarl dropped his voice; jerked his head towards the cabin where Ylana lay. "Stay with her, Ungo. We can't afford to lose her."

"The men—"

"Would you chance it? Would you trust that much to them?"

For a moment their eyes clashed. But the questions held their own bleak answers. Muttering, half-sullen, the big Jovian moved aside.

Jarl said: "I'll be back, Ungo." Silently, he dropped out the hatch to the ground and strode towards the dim lights that marked the ancient, scabrous buildings, which fringed the port.

But every step was a coal for the dull fire of tension that burned within him. Would he really be back? Would he ever see the carrier again, or Ungo?

Or Ylana...

He wondered.

THE native quarter closed in about him, heavy with the stench of age and rotting garbage. *Vocorn* pipes wailed, thin and minor, and strange eyes stared at him, luminous in the descending night. Once he stepped shuddering into the protoplasmic slime of some primitive life form as it writhed its way across the mud-choked cobbles; once, through a doorway, he glimpsed a snake-woman's sinuous dancing in the light of flaring *thes*-wood torches.

But he hurried on, still wrapped and trapped in his own dark thoughts.

Again and again, in spite of him, his mind flashed back to Wassreck...Ktar Wassreck, tortured genius, who'd come for him at Horla.

Could betrayal find a haven in such a man?

Jarl Corvett cursed aloud. It was beyond the believing.

Yet if it were true...

A chill shook Jarl. Where did loyalty lie, in man or duty?

Especially if that duty were only to a dream, the way of the raider...

He could find no answer. Savagely, he kicked a whimpering *Bok* from his path and pushed on through the darkness.

And Sais...what of her? Would he find her waiting, or vanished? What would she say? How could he tell her?

Tight-jawed, head down, he hurried on the faster.

Then, at last, he was striding out into the Place of the Raiders...crossing the open court to his own quarters.

He tried the door.

It was locked. Angrily, he beat on it with a heavy fist.

A rustle of sound came from within. The door opened a crack.

Belligerently, Jarl shoved inside.

A hard object gouged his back. By sheer reflex, he tried to leap aside, to whirl.

But rough hands seized him. A powerful arm jerked back his head, the wrist-bone jammed so hard against his throat that he choked and gasped for breath, his struggles unavailing. Close to his ear, a rough voice rasped, "Give up, you *zanat*, or I'll break your neck!"

Already the blackness was swimming with sparks and stars. Reeling, Jarl called a halt to battle.

"That's better!" the voice rasped. And then: "All right! We've got him! Let's have some light!"

The inner door opened. A yellow glare flooded the entryway. Staggering, arms locked behind him, Jarl was dragged into the room beyond.

Blinking, he stared into familiar faces...the cold, hard-bitten faces of the chieftains of the raider fleet—Toran the *Malya*...the mongrel, Tas Karrel...Bor Legat of Mercury...half-a-dozen others.

And there was another with them, not a warrior...one who's dark, proud, lovely face was pale beneath its color.

Jarl choked, "Sais—! What have they done to you—?"

THE woman who was *Ktar* Wassreck's daughter pulled together the torn bodice of her kirtle. A sudden flush replaced her pallor. "Ask them, Jarl." The fine, dark eyes with which she swept the raider chiefs were bitter, scornful.

Jarl stood very still. Cold-eyed, seething, he looked from one captain to another.

He said tightly: "You know this woman. You know she's under my protection. Who among you saw fit to lay hands on her, in my own quarters?" And then, with special, deadly emphasis: "Who *dared* to do it?"

But the chieftains' eyes threw back his fury. Their faces stayed hard, bleak, impassive.

"You *starbos!*" Jarl lashed. "Are you afraid to talk? Have you left your tongues on Pluto?"

The chiefs exchanged glances. Then, almost idly, Bor Legat moved forward—Bor Legat of Mercury, Bor Legat the ruthless. His lean body's shell-plates clacked in the stillness like tiny castanets. The basilisk eyes were like diamonds.

"Corvett," he said gently, "we're not afraid. Maybe this will convince you."

One arm appendage whipped up. The splayed, tentacular digits stung Jarl's face like flicking lashes.

Jarl rocked in a red haze of fury. "Bor Legat—"

"I know. You'll kill me." Chill, casual, the Mercurian crossed to the chart table and slouched down on one radial hip.

The tentacular digits wrapped around the proton grenade that served as a chart-weight and swung it idly to and fro.

To Jarl, the ticking seconds were like eons. The tension rising in the room was almost a living thing. He waited, not speaking.

At last Bor Legat raised the basilisk eyes to him. "Word travels fast, Corvett. We know you've got *rey* Gundre's daughter."

Jarl stared. "That's why you're here—?"

The Mercurian shrugged. "What else? And what better place to trap you than your own quarters?"

The other raiders nodded.

"And Sais—?" Jarl queried tightly.

"We needed her, to force your hand."

Jarl shot a quick glance at the woman. She stood as before, straight and proud, one hand to her bodice. Her dark eyes spoke unreadable volumes.

Bor Legat laughed softly. "She wants your help, Corvett. I hope that she'll get it."

JARL turned on him, voice raw and scalding. "Quit talking in riddles! What is it you're after?"

"You're not that stupid, Corvett." The Mercurian swung the proton grenade a fraction faster. "We want the girl, of course; Gundre's daughter, Ylana."

"Why?"

"To drive a bargain." The faintest hint of urgency crept into Legat's tone. "We know why you stole her. You're out to save Wassreck."

"And you—?" Jarl put scorn into his voice.

"Death comes to all raiders. Why should a traitor's tale be different?" The Mercurian lowered the grenade and leaned forward. "You can have it straight, Corvett: *rey* Gundre's made us an offer. If we give him you and Ylana, he'll spare Ceresta."

"And you believe him——?" Jarl laughed harshly. "No wonder you came here! You're mad as a *ban*, Legat! How long do you think he'd hold to his promise?"

"Long enough," the Mercurian clipped curtly. He sat back once more. Again, idly, he swung the grenade like a deadly oval pendulum.

Jarl said: "Maybe there are some things you don't know—about Wassreck; about his new projector—"

"Yes; we've heard about it." A veil of craft and malice drew over the basilisk eyes. "You see, we've got it, too, Corvett."

Jarl started. "You've got it——?"

"You heard me." Bor Legat's smile grew to a ghoulish grin, leering and macabre. "Sais gave it to us."

"Sais—!" Jarl swung sharply.

The woman's ripe lips quivered. Once more her color deepened. "Yes, Jarl. I knew the secret. I gave it to them."

For a long, taut moment, Jarl studied her. But as before, the dark eyes were unfathomable.

He turned back to Bor Legat. "So what are your plans?"

"You can guess them, can't you?" the Mercurian chuckled. "All we need is time. You'll buy that for us—you, and the girl, Ylana. Then, when the Federation fleet strikes through the Belt to blast us, we'll have a surprise of our own all ready and waiting for them."

"I see." Jarl nodded slowly, but his mind was racing. Then, pouring savage scorn into his voice, he lashed out at the raiders: "Are you utter fools, you *chitzas*? Do you rate *rey* Gundre as a moonstruck idiot?" He laughed, harsh and curt. "He'll strike, all right; but not the way you expect, nor by the path you hope for! He'll know from the start that you plan to trap him! His ships will break through before you have the chance to trap them—"

HE slashed on, in that vein; and as he talked he could see doubt flare in the chieftains' eyes. Tas Karrel's glance wavered. Toran the *Malya* frowned and shifted.

But Bor Legat the ruthless did not shift or waver.

"We'll chance that," he clipped; and in spite of their doubts, the others nodded.

Jarl's jaw set hard. "Play it that way, then, if you can." He jerked free of the hands that held him; hooked his thumbs in his belt in a gesture of cold defiance. *"If* you can…"

Bor Legat's arm came down. The proton bomb swung loose at his side as he leaned forward. "If—?" he queried, too gently.

Jarl said: "You need two prisoners to keep your traitor bargain. You've only got one."

"You mean, you won't give up the girl." The Mercurian was almost purring. "We counted on your being stubborn, Corvett. That's why we held your lovely Sais a prisoner. With her to help, I think we can convince you."

With an effort, Jarl held his face immobile. He did not speak.

Bor Legat said: "Torture means little to a man like you, Jarl Corvett. I doubt that it would break you. But if you knew your silence would doom this woman…"

Sais cried: "No, Jarl—!" Before they could stop her, she was running to him. She threw her arms around him. "Jarl, they're mad with fear of my father's weapon! If you give *rey* Gundre's daughter to them, they will gamble the fate of the outlaw worlds on their bargain with him—!"

For a moment Jarl held her to him. Her warmth, the softness of her body, brought new strain, new tension. The fragrance of her dark hair stabbed like a knife-blade.

Slouched on the chart table, Bor Legat smiled and swung the proton grenade. "Well, Corvett?"

Again Jarl looked from one raider to another. But their hard faces showed no trace of mercy, no hint of indecision.

Bleakly, he turned back to Bor Legat.

The Mercurian set the proton bomb down on the table with a thud. A grim finality was in the gesture.

"We've got three Earth days, Corvett," he said in a flat, hard voice. "Three days to turn you over to *rey* Gundre." And then:

"It could seem three thousand years to your lovely Sais, if you stay stubborn."

ONCE more, the seconds dragged like eons. Again Jarl looked to the raider chiefs, the burly crewmen.

A thought moiled in the far reaches of his brain: *If I could only snatch a weapon...*

But even as it came, it died again. What good could any weapon do against so many? Even if he killed Bor Legat, there'd be the others.

The Mercurian said: "We're wasting time, Corvett. Give us Ylana—or we'll get to work on your own woman."

Sais choked, "Jarl, stand firm—! Let them have me; it doesn't matter..."

Her voice broke. Jarl held her tighter. Bitterly, he thought of Wassreck, her father, and of Horla.

What was loyalty now, when it made a man try to choose between Sais and the thin-drawn chance that he might somehow save Ceresta?

Of a sudden he felt as if he were being pulled apart by the conflicting claims of love and loyalty, torn asunder under the impact of a dozen different kinds of duty.

The proton bomb on the table would rend a man less.

The proton bomb...

Bor Legat straightened. He snapped to the crewmen, "Take the woman!"

Never had the basilisk eyes held more deadly malice.

"Jarl..." whispered Sais. But her voice held only proud farewell; no tears nor fears, no piteous entreaty.

A raider gripped her shoulder.

Jarl said, "Wait..."

He spoke to Bor Legat, but his eyes were on the grenade that stood beside the Mercurian on the table. A tremor of chill fascination touched him as he stared at the safety pin, the firing lever.

"A change of heart—?" Legat smiled his ghoulish smile. "For a moment, there, I thought you'd let us have the woman."

"No, Bor," Jarl Corvett said tightly, and in that moment a raider's own wild recklessness was singing in him. "I've other plans for Sais, and you. If they work, she'll live, and so will I— and you, you scum, there'll come a day when you'll have your chance to die by inches!"

"What—?" Bor Legat came erect, as if he could not believe the words he heard.

Sais' eyes went wide. She tried to push back from Jarl.

A raider crewman reached for his arm.

"You heard me right," Jarl Corvett said. He let his shoulders slump and made as if to turn away. Of a sudden his muscles were tense to aching.

The crewman stretched to clutch him.

But Jarl moved faster. Catching Sais about the waist, he flung her bodily against the raider. Then, whirling, he lunged for the proton bomb on the table.

Bor Legat snatched for his pistol.

But Jarl smashed an elbow into his middle.

THE Mercurian retched and reeled. Before he could recover, Jarl drove past him—clawing the grenade up from the table, jerking out the pin.

"Corvett, no—!" shrieked a raider. Another whipped up a ray gun.

Jarl spun about. His hand ached with the strain of holding down the spring of the bomb's curved firing lever.

But fierce exhilaration surged within him. With a shout he swung the grenade high above his head, where all could see. "Look, *chitzas!*"

One and all, they froze in their tracks, eyes suddenly aglisten with the glassy sheen of fear. Even Sais' dark, lovely face was all at once a mirror of panic.

"Shoot, curse you!" Jarl cried, and his voice rang with fierce triumph, with exultation. "Shoot and be damned! Because if I die, I'll take you with me!"

Bor Legat choked, "Corvett—!"

Jarl whirled upon him. "Yes, you *starbo!* Take me! But remember—if I let go this firing lever, the spring completes the contact for me!"

"No—!" croaked Legat, and his shell-like body plates were clacking. "No, Corvett! That thing would blast us all to atoms!"

Jarl said, "That's better." Coolly, he lowered the bomb and held it cradled between his hands. "Sais…"

"Yes, Jarl…" Quickly, supply, she moved forward.

"We're leaving now," Jarl clipped.

And then, to the chieftains: "You want to live? Don't follow."

Hate hammered at him, a living thing—the hate of the wolf pack that sees its prey escaping. Fists clenched, and gun-hands quivered, and eyes drew to murderous, icy diamonds.

Jarl laughed aloud—scornful, contemptuous. The woman at his side, looking neither to right nor left, he strode to and through the door; closed it behind him.

Sais' taut whisper cut through the darkness: "Jarl, they'll come after us! They'll shoot at a distance—"

Wordless, heart racing, he pushed her forward faster. She stumbled across the final threshold, out into the night and the Place of the Raiders.

Jarl threw a quick glance back. Already, behind them, the door to the inner room was opening.

Cursing, he lobbed the proton grenade back over his shoulder; then bolted after Sais.

The night exploded into crashing chaos. A wall of force smashed Jarl to the cobbles. Screams and shrieks slashed through dust and smoke and falling debris.

But he was outside, the wall between him and the blast. Scrambling to his feet, he dragged Sais up.

Together, they raced for the blackness of the native quarter…

CHAPTER SIX

THEY ran through the murk of Ceres' night till their lungs caught fire, and their eyes rolled up, and their quaking legs could no longer hold them.

Then, at last, sobbing and panting, they fell in a heap in a rubble-strewn alley, heedless of time or place or peril.

But that passed, too. Slowly, the pain and weariness ebbed. Jarl's strength flowed back. Once more, he was acutely conscious of the filth, the smells, the slithering vermin. Somewhere afar, the *vocorn* pipes still were wailing.

Sais twisted against him, her ripe body smooth as rippling velvet. When he rested his palm on her hip, she gripped it fiercely in the darkness. Her hand was hot; he could feel the movement of her quickened breathing.

The muscles in Jarl's belly drew tight. All at once—even here, even now—he could think of nothing save this woman. His fingers trembled as he smoothed her dark hair; touched her eyes, her lips.

She moved closer, till the curve of her cheek lay against his shoulder. The pressure of her body was a silent pledge, an invitation.

Sais… She was all passion, all woman.

And all his.

Or was she?

The question came without his bidding. In spite of it. Yet once it had come, it would not go away.

He shifted. But it did no good. The spell of her was upon him, melded of her, woman's flesh and fragrance.

She pressed closer.

Rigid, he fought a silent battle…and prayed that he would lose it.

Why did he hang back? How could he doubt her?

But in his heart he knew the answer to all his questions.

This woman whose touch made his heart beat faster was more than merely woman. She was Sais herself, *Ktar* Wassreck's daughter.

Once, that had been a bond between them.

Now it rose like a cold stone wall, setting them apart.

Because now, in spite of himself, in spite of loyalty or duty, he doubted Wassreck...

A *Pervod's* drunken laugh drifted to Jarl, dull and muffed. The faint, alluring scent of *mafrak* reached his nostrils.

Sais' fingers brushed his throat.

He could stand the strain no longer. Twisting, he pushed her back. "Sais..." Even in a whisper, his voice was raw and rasping.

He could feel her body stiffen. "Yes, Jarl...?"

How could he say it? What words could he find?

He blurted: "They said on Vesta that your father had...surrendered."

For an instant her shoulders stayed tight and straining. Then, incredibly, the tension left them.

"Yes, Jarl." Her voice was the barest murmur. "They told it true. He sent a secret message to *rey* Gundre..."

A NUMBNESS crept through Jarl Corvett. He could hear his own heart pounding in the stillness. "But why, Sais? Why? How could he do it—?"

And her whisper came back: "You mean—you thought he had betrayed you?"

The hurt in her voice twisted at Jarl Corvett. But he threw it off; forced himself to press her further: "You ask—when for his own gain he left you here, to die with the rest of us on Ceres?"

He felt her body quiver, and it was like a knife-stab in his belly.

But when she spoke, scorn edged her words: "You'd believe that, after Horla?"

"What can I believe—?" He broke off; lashed out: "If he didn't, tell me! Why did he go? Why did he use you to bait me into a trap that almost snared me?"

A new tremor ran through Sais' smooth, perfect body. Of a sudden she reached out and once more gripped his clenched fist in the darkness. "Jarl, believe me…"

"Believe you—?"

"The trap was my fault, not his. He sent me a message that came too late. You'd gone before I found it…" She choked. "Now I must tell you all—"

"All—?"

"Yes, no matter what I promised." Sais broke off, still trembling; then hurried on. "The projector…it was a gamble…"

Again she fumbled, halted. Jarl waited in taut silence.

She said: "It draws its power from cosmic dust."

"I know."

"But that was only half my father's secret!" Sais' voice took on a new raw edge. "Did you ever ask yourself how my father learned to utilize that power, Jarl Corvett? Did you ever wonder why it was he who mastered its principle, after the finest scientists of every planet had striven for a thousand years and failed?"

Jarl frowned in the darkness. "You mean—?"

"I mean that it was not he who solved the problem!" Sais' nails bit into his hand. Her voice lost its edge in an eager rush of words. "Jarl, the secret came from another race—from a people who voyaged across the void…perhaps from even beyond the stars! Eons ago, they lived and died. But one of their ships had crashed on Vesta. That was why my father built his workshop there—so that he could better study what little they'd left behind them. There was a book with metal pages; he found it deep in the buried wreckage. From it, he worked out the plans for this new projector."

IT made Jarl's breath quicken, that picture—the picture of Wassreck, twisted genius, digging through dead ruins in spite of a tortured, pain-racked body. The endless hours, the weary years, the lightning mind and infinite patience—all were part of an old, familiar pattern.

Wassreck's pattern.

But it still was not enough to still the doubts that plagued him. With an effort, he held his voice flat and clipped, emotionless. "So...he gave this master secret to *rey* Gundre...

"He doomed the outlaw worlds. He left us to die here, at Ceresta."

"No! He did not!" Bitter vehemence rang in her denial. "You fool, the projector itself was nothing! He had to break through the Federation fleet's blockade in order to reach Venus' orbit, and then Womar—"

"Womar—!" Jarl went rigid. He strained his eyes to see the woman in the darkness.

"Yes. Womar, the satellite that hides behind the mother planet!" Sais writhed upright. Again her words came fast and eager. "There was another ship, Jarl Corvett—another craft built by that same ancient master race somewhere across the void! If my father can find it, it will mean the end of the Federation! It will buy the outlaw worlds their freedom!"

"But Womar..." Choking, Jarl came up beside her. His thin-stretched mask of bleakness fell away. "Sais, it's madness!"

"Because of the primitives, you mean? Because of the Federation ban, the deserts—?" Sais laughed aloud, and there was scorn and fury in it. "Yes, Jarl Corvett, its utter madness! That's why my father went in secret, leaving you behind to call him traitor! He wanted no other to die with him on such a hopeless quest. So he sent his message to *rey* Gundre, wagered his own life on the one slim, desperate chance that he could bring destruction to the Federation!"

The fears, the doubts...they all were dying. And as they died, a gnawing sickness grew in Jarl Corvett. Of a sudden he was himself traitor, betrayer, for his very doubting.

"But why—?" he whispered. "Why did he go, Sais? What secret could be greater than the one he gave to Gundre?"

Sais laughed again, more softly. Once more, she came close to him, as if unwilling, even here, to speak of this thing above a breathless murmur. "The robots, Jarl; the robots!"

He stared. "The robots—?"

"Yes!" Now her voice shook with excitement. "Jarl, they were no idle fancy, no toys brought to being out of an old man's dreams. They were models of warriors—the great, inanimate metal warriors of that alien race from beyond the stars. He built them from plans in the books he found in the wrecked ship."

FOR Jarl, it was as if a curtain had suddenly been pulled aside. His mind flashed back to Vesta, to Wassreck's workshop...back to the great hall's echoing vastness, and the towering metal monsters that, shoulder to shoulder, lined its walls.

Sais still was speaking: "He knew that the outlaw worlds were doomed, Jarl. The Federation was too strong. The projector—it was only another weapon. For victory, the raider fleet needed something more."

Jarl did not speak.

She said: "The metal warriors were to be that 'something more'. Not models, such as he constructed, but giants, monsters—huge creatures, indestructible, so mighty that they could break space ships in their hands." The woman's voice rose; took on a richer timbre. "Think of it, Jarl Corvett! Think of an army of those awful warriors, each alone strong enough to desolate a planet! What would power like that mean to the outlaw worlds—?"

She broke off, shaking. With an oath, Jarl pulled her to him; held her.

"But he failed, Jarl..." Sais' words came dull and muffled. "He could not give them life."

"You mean—?"

"The control was a mystery he could not master. The books told nothing of its workings."

"So now he would go to Womar…"

"Yes. There was a chance, he thought that he might find the secret there, where the other alien ship had fallen. He had a theory that the primitives themselves were decadent descendants of the master race."

"But Womar…" Jarl's voice trailed off. He thought of the tales he'd heard, the things he'd seen. Of Venus' hidden satellite and its deserts. Of the Federation ban that made it death to land there. Of the beings behind that ban, the primitives, still unconquered, with their savagery and lust for blood and darkly rumored rites.

Tremulous, close to him, Sais whispered, "He gambled his life, Jarl Corvett. In secret, in order that he would not risk yours nor mine."

In the distance, Jarl still could hear the wailing *vocorn* pipes; the shouts, the shrieks, the drunken laughter. A *thes*-wood torch was a flaring pinpoint in the blackness. He rolled the acrid taste of Rogek gas about his tongue…drank in the *Mah'ham's* stench.

Yes, this was Ceres, a Cerestan night, and he was here, with the warmth and softness of dark Sais pressed against him.

Yet another part of him was far away…far, far away in time and space and circumstance, armoring his quivering belly in a surface plate of boldness as he strode out on Horla to face the agony of the flame-death.

And there was Wassreck, too, *Ktar* Wassreck, with his burning eyes and pain-racked body, blasting down through the holocaust to save him.

Loyalty…it was such a feeble, tenuous thing.

Yet the bonds it forged were stronger than telonium or steel.

Again he cursed, and pushed Sais back. Catching her hand, he turned and led her, stumbling, through the darkness.

"Jarl…"

He clipped: "We're going to the space-port. *rey* Gundre's carrier waits for us there."

"And then—?"

"We blast for Womar."

"Jarl—!"

He strode on faster—hurrying, giving her no answer. There were too many things to say...too many words he could not utter.

THEY left the alley for another, broader. A *dau* brushed past them in the murk. Two bulbous Thorians parted, moving out of their way. Curious, glowing eyes of *llorin* watched them from an entryway.

Then, around another turn, the buildings thinned. The odor of Rogek gas and rocket fuel grew stronger.

And, ahead, a shadowy group moved from one looming bulk of structure to another.

Jarl jerked Sais back into the blackness that rimmed a cone-like *Pervod* dwelling.

"Jarl—"

He clapped a hand across Sais' mouth. "Quiet! Bor Legat's men may still be here before us!"

Jarl felt a tremor run through her. Ghost-silent, he led the way along the building; then, after a moment's pause, ran on swiftly to an ancient *Fantay* structure.

The shadow-group ahead was breaking up...spreading out in a thin black line of menace.

Tight-nerved, Jarl drew Sais to the right, parallel to the skirmish line, along the crumbling *Fantay* spire...then on through the burrow-like workings of the spider-men of Rhea, past flat-roofed habitat of the *llorin*.

They came out into another alley.

But ahead, here, too, he caught a glimpse of motion, the hint of a far-flung raider cordon.

They tried again, by another alley—the one down which Jarl had come when he left the carrier. He almost imagined he could make out the ship's slim silver form far off in the vastness of the port, in spite of the obscuring night.

But again, between them and the sprawling ramping-place, stood sinister figures.

Jarl rested his shoulders against the wall of a rambling *fala* hostel. He felt old beyond belief; incredibly weary. His muscles ached with tension.

Sais touched his arm. "Jarl…" Her voice was a ragged whisper.

He sucked in air. "Wait here a moment."

Once more, in dead silence, he moved forward, skirting the pool of greenish glow that marked the hostel's entry. Cat-footed, taut, he made his way along the wall towards the port, the shadowy-figures.

Only then, without warning, a spear of light lanced through the darkness. An energy-bolt splintered stone bare inches from his shoulder.

He dived back by instinct; landed running.

In the same instant a cry went up—the wild hunting-cry of Bor Legat's raiders.

Jarl caught Sais' hand and dashed for the corner of the building.

From behind them came a pelting rush of feet, a babble of fierce, life-thirsting voices. The night blazed with the fire of raider weapons.

Barely in time, they made the corner. Panting, they lunged on into the maze of alleys.

But then, ahead of them, rose other voices. New figures loomed; new weapons flamed and echoed.

Jarl catapulted Sais into an entryway. Savagely, he kicked at the door's lock.

THE door burst open. Beyond lay the blackness of an ebon sack, thick enough to cut. The air that puffed out was stale and dead, heavy with a musty smell of age, abandonment, disintegration.

Jarl pushed inside and heeled the door shut. The clamor of the alley faded.

Breathing hard he groped through the room. Thick dust scuffed up beneath his feet. Sais clung to his hand, fingers slick with icy sweat. "Which way—?" She was half-sobbing.

"Up!" Jarl clenched his teeth. "There's got to be a stair, a ladder!"

They felt their way through another room. Another, and another.

Then: "Jarl—! I've found it!"

Jarl wheeled, moving to her. He touched the edge of worn stone steps. "Come on!"

They climbed through the murk, and Jarl thought of *quirsts* and *hwins*—a thousand deadly, crawling, nameless horrors. But there was no other way, no faintest chance. Tight-jawed, he shoved his thoughts back and stumbled higher.

Three levels they climbed. Then the stone steps ended. Numb, rigid, Jarl felt his way to an outer room.

Stars shone faintly through a window. Sais still at his heels, he crossed to the casement and looked out.

Far below, the shouts and curses of Bor Legat's men still echoed.

But Jarl paid them no heed. He had eyes only for the flat-topped *llorin* dwelling that crowded next to this structure in which he had found temporary haven.

The *llorin*-pile's roof rose to within short feet of the window. Beyond it lay another; then a *Fantay* spire…

Again he said, "Come on!" and levered open the window.

New agitation gleamed in Sais' eyes, but she moved forward, wordless.

Cat-like, Jarl dropped to the *llorin* roof. After a moment's hesitation, Sais followed.

Silent, nerves raw with tension, they picked a path along the beams to the next building and crossed to it.

Here even the beams were rotten, sagging. Testing with his foot at each step, Jarl led the way around the outer wall to the spire beyond.

Even at its lowest point, the edge of the *Fantay* peak was feet above Jarl's head, across a yawning two-foot gap that plunged chasm-like to the ground so far below.

Bleakly, Jarl studied it; measured the distance with his eye. "Up, Sais..." He lifted her; tottered precariously against the rim of coping while, whole body atremble, she balanced on his broad shoulders.

She whispered, "Jarl, I'll never make it..." Her words died in a quavering sound of pure hysteria.

A TRICKLE of sweat dripped from Jarl's chin. He dug his fingers into her ankles till her blood spurted and ran down his nails. "You'll make it..."

"No, Jarl—! No! I can't—!"

The sweat dripped faster. Jarl could feel Sais' terror. It crawled in her voice and breath and body, quaked and quivered in the very air.

But behind there was only the tender mercy of Bor Legat's raiders.

Ahead, at least they had a faint slim chance to reach the carrier.

The carrier...so near, and yet so far.

Through clenched teeth, he said, "You'll make it—or I'll drop you down the crack!"

He tilted her forward.

For an instant she hung there. He could hear a scream rising in her throat.

Jarl Corvett died a thousand deaths.

Then out she swung, high over the chasm. Instinctively, her hands shot out...caught the *Fantay* spire's low-dipping edge...clung there...

He said tightly: "Pull yourself up! I'll help you!" Bracing himself, straining every muscle, he lifted her higher...higher...till her feet were at arm's length above his head.

Panting, crying, she pulled herself half onto the spire.

He let go her feet.

She gasped in new panic. But her grip held firm. Twisting, spasmodically, she swung her feet up and lay there, sobbing.

Jarl's muscles went weak as water.

But he did not dare to hesitate. Stiffly, he swung onto the knee-high coping; crouched there.

The chasm below drew his eyes like a magnet. He tore them away; forced himself to look up, instead, to the spire. Sucking in air, he poised himself, tensing.

Sais stared down at him. Something close akin to horror was in her eyes.

With all his might, Jarl leaped upward, outward, straining to reach the other wall.

One hand touched—and slipped.

The other hooked round the edge of the stone ledge above.

Sais clutched his free hand and tried to lift him. With a desperate effort, he twisted and lunged again, hanging there in space.

This time he got a grip on the ledge's inner edge. Sais tugged at his tunic's collar. Gasping for breath, he levered himself higher, up onto his elbows. A final surge carried him out of the chasm.

Sais sank down beside him. For a long moment they lay there—both panting, both shaking.

But there was no time for weakness. Lurching to his feet, Jarl began working his way around the rim.

THEY moved on to new buildings—one, two, half-a-dozen...always striving in the direction of the port.

Then, at last, they reached a final, ramshackle structure only one level high.

Beyond it, the ramping-place stretched off through the flare-sparked blackness of the night.

Jarl peered down into the flanking alleys. But this time he could find no shadow-cordon, no trace of Legat's raiders.

Sais brushed against him. Once more, he caught the half-forgotten fragrance of her hair.

He pressed her hand. "It looks good, Sais. Legat never thought about the roofs. His men are farther back in the quarter."

"Then——?"

"We'll chance it."

Her lips touched his cheek. It was her only answer.

Together, hand in hand, they slipped down a rickety outside ramp to the ground. In silence, they made their way across the sprawling port's scorched cinders.

As they walked, Jarl felt the surface tension leave him. The heavy, mixed smells of Rogek gas and rocket fuel were perfume in his nostrils. His job was done, here at Ceresta. He'd rescued Sais and learned the truth about *Ktar* Wassreck.

Now, he could almost laugh when he thought of Legat.

But underneath, a stronger conflict plagued him. Because, again, it was his destiny to go forth to battle…to lead good men, good friends, to die for the cause of the raider worlds, and loyalty.

Frowning, he thought of Wassreck and of Womar…the giant robots. Of Ungo and Ylana.

As for himself, how long could his luck hold? When, at long last, would fate decide to down him?

Shrugging, he veered his course in the direction of a massive marker pylon. What did it matter, when he fell? As Legat had said, death came to all raiders.

For now, it was enough that he should carve his way and do his duty.

Beside him, Sais asked, "How far is it, Jarl? I—I'm so tired."

"Only a little way. Just beyond the pylon." He put his arm about her.

"I'm glad…" She leaned upon him.

Jarl veered again. They rounded the corner of the marker.

"Where is it, Jarl?" Sais asked in a weary voice. And then: "Jarl! What's the matter?"

But Jarl hardly heard her. He stood stock-still, staring—
unable to move, unable to speak.

"Jarl—!"

He jerked free of the spell of shock; peered this way and that
in a frenzy of desperation. Once again, his heart was pounding.

But the cindered ramping-place stayed bare and echoing and
empty.

Carrier and crew alike had vanished!

CHAPTER SEVEN

JARL picked Tas Karrel's ship, the *Knife*. Unswerving, Sais at
his side, he stalked up her ramp.

A grim, slim, deadly craft, the *Knife*, black as the heart of her
mutant master. The fastest ship in all the raider fleet, with a
killer crew drawn from the scum of the whole wide solar system.

The guard at the hatch was such a one—an Earthman, long
fled from his own home planet. Slouched at his post below the
scarlet signal light, thumb hooked in belt, he stared bleakly off
across Ceresta's port and puffed at a *chang* cigarette of Venus.

Jarl's footsteps echoed. The guard swung round.

The next instant he was whipping up his blaster. The
cigarette fell from his lips, forgotten. "Jarl Corvett—!"

Jarl laughed, a cold and mirthless laugh, and raised his empty
hands. "Put your blaster down. I've come to see Tas Karrel."

"He's not aboard." The Earthman's blaster did not waver.

"I know it. I'll wait."

The guard's brow furrowed. For a moment he stood
hesitating, wordless.

Heedless of the menace in the cold blue eyes, Jarl brushed on
past him. Chill arrogance in his stance, he strode down the
echoing corridor to the crewmen's day room.

A knot of lounging raiders looked up as he entered then
snatched for weapons. Again his name rang: "Jarl Corvett!"
"It's Corvett!"

And again Jarl laughed his reckless laugh. "That's right. It's Corvett."

A *Pervod* pushed forward. Jarl recognized him as one of Tas Karrel's chief lieutenants.

The creature's chill reptilian eyes flicked from Jarl to Sais, then on to the Earthman guard who had followed them in. "What brings these two here? Where did they come from?"

"How should I know?" the Earthman shrugged. "They say they want Karrel—and I know he wants them."

"Yes. They find it easier to come than to leave us." The *Pervod* laughed harshly and swung back to Jarl. "You, Corvett! We know you! What do you want here?"

Bleakly, Jarl met the reptilian's glare. Feet wide apart, hands on hips, he stood straight and steady, surveying the crewmen who crowded around him.

"I want you!" he slashed harshly.

"Me—?" He could see the lean *Pervod* stiffen...

Jarl let his voice ring. "Yes, you—and all of these others. The *Knife*, too..."

He grinned as he said it, and looked from one hard-bitten face to another—measuring each raider, timing his pause to their grim, deadly potential. He knew them so well; these outlaw crewmen. *Chonya* and *Malya*; *Pervod* and Earthman; *dau*, *fala*, *Fantay*—they were one with him. When his eyes met theirs, it was almost as if he could see their restless minds working.

A SILENCE built up in the echoing day room. Before it could break, he spoke again to them:

"I need a ship!" he said boldly. "A fighting ship, fast enough to break through the Federation's own cordon. And"—he paused—"that ship must have a crew that fears no one."

The silence echoed louder.

He said: "The *Knife* is the fastest ship in the raider fleet—and a crew that will raid with Tas Karrel would spit in *rey* Gundre's own eye!"

Still, for a moment, the silence hung upon them. Then, slowly at first, but rising, a ripple of wry, bleak laughter ran through the crowd.

He knew that he had them, then. He leaned forward…let his voice drop to a confidential note. "What does a raider want most, my comrades? Loot? *Kabat*? Women—?"

He grinned again, as he said 'women', and lifted a hand to dark Sais' velvet shoulder.

She twisted. The laughter rippled louder.

Jarl planted his foot on a chair; rested elbow on knee. "Yes, we all want them, my comrades. But"—he dropped his voice still lower—"so do other men."

The raiders crowded closer, craning and straining to hear.

"Then where's the difference, between us and those others—?" Abruptly, he straightened and brought up his fist. He threw his words at them, in a fierce, ringing challenge: "The difference—? I'll tell you, comrades! It's not loot that we raid for, nor *kabat*, nor women; not really! It's freedom we are after—the freedom to roam the void as free men should, and to hell with the thrice-cursed tyrants of the Federation!"

Now the crewmen, too, shouted, in wild exultation. The din echoed and deafened.

"Are you with me—?" Jarl roared.

But the *Pervod* leaped forward. "You dogs! What of Karrel?"

The shouting died down. Again all eyes came to Jarl Corvett.

He held the smile on his face. "Yes. What of Tas Karrel?"

The *Pervod's* claws crept towards his gun-butt. The bony wings whispered in the sudden stillness.

Very softly, Jarl said, "There's the law of the raiders. A chieftain must meet any man who dares challenge." And then: "You, *Pervod*! Will you fight hand-to-hand for Tas Karrel?"

The reptilian's eyes glinted. His claws touched the ray gun.

Scorn rang in Jarl's laugh. "I said hand-to-hand, by the law of the raiders! I came here unarmed, to fight Karrel to the death for his chiefship!"

A low mutter rose from the crewmen. The *Pervod's* eyes wavered.

Jarl said: "Know my pledge, comrades! Not booty, but freedom! If you blast with me, we may all die on Womar. If that doesn't suit you, kill me now, before I meet Karrel!"

The *Pervod* lieutenant's eyes sought out the crewmen. They shifted, not speaking.

Jarl laughed without mirth. "You see, *chitza*—? They want blood—mine, or Tas Karrel's!"

The reptilian looked away—past Jarl, to the doorway. His claws were atremble.

Then, visibly, he stiffened.

Jarl spun around.

TAS Karrel himself stood framed in the entry. His tiny, round, lidless eyes flamed green murder. "You *starbo*—!"

Tas Karrel, the mutant. Broad, tall, heavy-bodied. Hairy as a *dau*, and with a *dau's* bulging muscles. But his face was the blank, hairless face of the *Fantay*... without nose, without cheekbones.

"Welcome, Karrel!" Jarl laughed again, loud and reckless. "I'm claiming the *Knife* and your chiefship, by the law of the raiders!"

"A fight to the death—?" The other's lipless gash mouth twisted awry. The green eyes were smoldering. "A pleasure, Jarl Corvett!"

The huge mutant stripped off his tunic, his gun-belt.

His *Pervod* lieutenant cried, "Raiders! A death-ring!"

The crewmen fell back, and linked arms, formed a circle.

Knee-long arms swaying, their chief shambled forward.

Jarl pushed Sais back. The circle parted to pass her.

Karrel's mouth worked. "Jarl Corvett..."

"Yes."

"If you die, I claim the woman!"

Jarl's heart pounded. "If I die, you can have her!" He did not dare look at Sais.

The mutant moved into the circle. His prehensile fingers flexed and worked. His blank, grey-white face was a bleak mask of menace, the more fearsome for its very lack of expression.

Slowly, they moved around, ever facing—each searching for an opening, seeking some hint of weakness. The tension climbed higher, in a throbbing crescendo.

Jarl could feel the sweat come to his palms. His pulses hammered.

Then; suddenly, arms flailing, Tas Karrel sprang forward.

Jarl leaped back; jarred against the *Pervod* lieutenant.

Karrel lunged again. Again, Jarl tried to leap aside.

But a clawed Pervod foot hooked out and tripped him. He sprawled on the floor.

In a flash, Tas Karrel was upon him. A bulging *dau* arm bore down on his windpipe.

Writhing, Jarl tried to tear free. But the arm would not let him. The prehensile fingers gouged at his eyeballs.

He twisted; rocked back. Bit down on a finger.

Karrel jerked. Jarl bit harder. Lunging, he bucked the mutant forward...hooked a hammering heel up and around, into the blank *Fantay* face.

It was Karrel's turn to rock back. The hairy arm lifted.

Jarl brought his chin forward, sucking air in great, choking gulps. He drove a savage blow home below the other's rib casing.

Karrel tottered. Jarl broke clear; staggered upright.

The mutant threw himself round; started to lunge up.

Jarl kicked him in the face with all his might.

Karrel's head snapped back. His hand clutched for Jarl's ankle.

SAVAGELY, Jarl stomped down on the fingers. He smashed rights and lefts to the grey-white mask face. A cut opened. Grey-green ooze spurted.

Jarl kicked for the belly.

An incoherent cry burst from the gash-mouth. The mutant threw himself over, tumbling towards the edge of the circle.

A hoarse murmur rose from the crewmen. Wolf-like, arms still linked, they hunched forward.

Jarl's arms dragged like anchors. His ears rang; his lungs burned. Dimly, he saw Sais' panic-straut face at the edge of the circle. The sour stink of his own sweat rolled up in his nostrils.

But he dared not hold back. If Karrel rose, he was finished.

He dived in for the kill.

But the mutant was twisting. His feet smashed at Jarl's breastbone.

Jarl crashed back, dear to the other side of the circle.

Tas Karrel surged upright. "A knife—!" he roared harshly.

The *Pervod* flipped him a dagger. Swaying, he caught it...lunged for Jarl.

It was over. Jarl knew it. There was nothing he could do now.

Nothing but die.

The frenzy of death alone brought him to his feet. He hurled himself at the mutant.

Tas Karrel swayed aside, green eyes burning. Jarl hurtled past him; landed sobbing against the *Pervod*.

The reptilian laughed shrilly. Letting go of the arms of the raiders who flanked him, he caught Jarl...shoved him back at Tas Karrel.

Blindly, Jarl clutched the *Pervod's* belt. His weight carried them both to the circle's center.

Cursing, Karrel slashed for him.

Jarl wrenched to one side. The knife laid open the *Pervod's* side.

The reptilian screamed. His bony vestigial wings flailed.

In the same instant, Jarl caught Karrel's knife-hand. With his last ounce of strength, he wrenched it till the bones cracked.

The knife fell.

Jarl scooped it up. The *Pervod* scrambled from his path.

Tas Karrel stumbled backward. Fear flared in the green eyes.

Teeth bared now, Jarl followed.

The mutant sagged. Then, with a wild cry, hairy body shaking, he whirled and threw himself over the linked arms of his crewmen, out of the circle. He lunged for the exit.

"No—!" A raider whipped up his blaster. "Death to you, coward!"

He fired. Tas Karrel sprawled on his face in the doorway.

The circle broke into chaos.

Jarl spun about, seeking the *Pervod*.

The reptilian was backing away, slinking towards another door.

"You *chitza*—!"

The *Pervod* stopped short.

"Take your knife with you!" Jarl shouted. He drew back the blade.

Face contorted, the Venusian clawed for his ray gun.

Like lightning, Jarl hurled the dagger. It sank to the hilt in the *Pervod's* throat. Threshing in his death-throes, the creature spilled forward.

Jarl gripped a stanchion. "To your stations!" he shouted. "We're blasting for Womar!"

Order came from the chaos. Sub-chiefs bellowed commands. Crewmen boiled out of the doorways.

Sais ran to Jarl's side. Her white cheeks were tear-smudged, but she smiled through her tears.

There was a ringing of bells, a clanging of hatches. A *fala* cried, "All's ready!"

"For Womar—!" Jarl echoed.

A muffled roar cut him short. The room rocked with the shock of the takeoff as the *Knife* slashed its way up from the port, out from Ceres.

Jarl threw one arm around Sais—more for support than from feeling. It was all he could do to stand upright.

She braced him. "You mean it—? We're going to Womar...?" All at once her voice trembled.

Shrugging, Jarl rested against her. "You heard my orders."

"But…what of Bor Legat…*rey* Gundre…?"

"We'll face that when we meet it." With an effort, Jarl straightened. "Now, I've got to rest."

"Of course, Jarl…" She moved close beside him, helping him as he limped to Tas Karrel's quarters.

Then they came to the cabin, and she, too, would have entered. But he barred her way. "No, Sais."

"Jarl…"

"No." He shook his head, closed the door. Heavily, he stumbled to a couch and dropped down.

But though Sais stayed behind, his own dark thoughts would not.

It was madness, this venture; what other name could a man find for a wild dash for Womar?

Yet what else could he do, with time running out on him? At best, he had three slim Earth days to save Ceres.

Three slim days, less the travel…

And Womar… What might he find when at last he ramped there? Suppose Wassreck was wrong, and there were no robots? Or if the metal monsters still lay hidden there, how much chance had he to find them?

As for fitting them for battle, mastering the controls that sent them forth…

HE shuddered, and his brow seemed suddenly burning hot, as with a fever. Then he chilled. Shaking, drawing covers close about him, he wondered if his wounds had drained him, sapped his strength too low.

But what chance did he have, unless, he went on to Womar?

What chance indeed, when even his own kind turned against him!

His own kind, the raiders. He knew them so well—how they felt, the twist, of their reckless, ice-edged thinking. And because he knew, it was not in him to hate them or betray them. No; at worst, he could only strive and fail.

And if he failed—? He cursed and twisted. *rey* Gundre would surely blast the raider fleet. The outlaw worlds would die.

Freedom would die with them.

Wassreck, too.

Three days only…for freedom, and for Wassreck…

Perhaps he slept, then. Or perhaps it was only delirium's distorted screen that drew the twisting patterns across his mind.

Whatever it was, it lifted brain from body…moved him up from Tas Karrel's couch—out of the room, the ship itself…across the void, through space and time. The hideous, shining masks of Womar's primitives hurtled down upon him out of swirling mists. Madly, he battled strange life forms in a world he'd never seen.

But he was not alone, for now other faces revolved past him slowly, crying fearful words he could not hear…Ungo's face; Ylana's…

Ylana—! The red lips smiled and mocked him as she beckoned, and her hair was a rippling pool of purest gold. There was the softness of her body pressed against him; the grey eyes, shadowy as silver pools.

Ungo. Ylana. Where were they? Why had they left him to die back there on Ceres? What could have taken them away?

Now Bor Legat's face came sweeping towards him, basilisk orbs twin mirrors of craft and malice. His body plates were rattling with his laughter—the merciless, cacophonic laughter of the Mercurian who sees his enemy fall and die.

Then another voice was calling, close beside him, and this time he could hear the words, even if he could not understand. They pulled him back across the void, up from the death and tumult of the unknown alien world.

Straining, struggling, he sought to place the tones, the timbre, and as he fought, it dawned upon him that it was Sais' voice, and that his eyes were closed.

His lids were leaden weights, but he dragged them up. Numbly, he forced Tas Karrel's room back into focus.

Sais stood beside him, face strained and drawn. Her words took on meaning: "Jarl—! Quick! Wake up—!"

He lurched from the couch. "What's the matter? What is it—?"

"Quiet—!" Panic was in her raw whisper. "You slept so long, Jarl! We're coming down now, ramping on Womar…"

He pushed back his hair; shook the haze from his eyes. "Then what—?"

"It's the crewmen." He could feel a tremor pass through her. Her eyes would not meet his. "I—I told them too much, Jarl. About Womar…the robots. Now they have sent for Bor Legat—"

"Bor Legat—!"

"Yes. They don't trust you. They plan to seize you and hold you…"

Jarl cursed. "No! It can't be—"

"What can I say, Jarl?" Her mouth quivered. "Beat me, if you want to—"

"No." His hands shook, but he fought down his fury…even forced a thin smile. "Maybe this way is better, Sais…"

SPINNING round, he snatched up a belt heavy with dead Tas Karrel's weapons and girded it about him.

The woman clutched his arm, eyes wide with new fear. "Jarl! What are you doing—?"

"What can I do?" He laughed harshly. "I'll drop down when we ramp and go on alone."

"No, Jarl—!"

"Yes! Stay in here. Lock the door, so they'll still think they've got me."

"No! You can't leave me!" Her voice rose. She was sobbing. "Please, Jarl! Take me with you—"

Jarl gripped her smooth shoulders fiercely; shook her. "Sais! Listen!" And then, as she quieted: "Sais, once before, I came down on Womar. I've seen the primitives." Involuntarily, he shuddered. "Believe me, Sais, no matter what the crew does to you, it can't match the work of those creatures."

"No, Jarl—"

A dim roar filled the room-the roar of a ramping. Walls and floor vibrated.

"Jarl, I'm going with you!"

The vibration stopped. The cabin echoed with sudden stillness as the great ship came to rest.

"Jarl…"

For the fraction of a second, Jarl hesitated. From afar, he could hear orders shouted. Once again, a knot drew tight in his belly.

"Please, Jarl…"

Pivoting, he stared down into Sais' tense, strained face.

Even now, she was lovely.

But he'd made his decision. There could be no other.

"Sais, I'm sorry…" He drove his clenched fist to the point of her jaw—a short, jarring blow.

He could see the shock glaze her eyes as her head snapped back. Her knees buckled.

"I'm sorry, Sais," he said again, even though he knew she could not hear. Ever so gently, he lowered her limp body to the couch.

He wondered if he'd ever see her again.

But it was no time for wondering, or thinking. He had a job to do, out there in the stretching, scorching, windswept deserts.

Silently, he eased open the cabin door.

The passageway outside was echoing, deserted.

Quick, quiet, he pulled the portal closed behind him and ran cat-footed for the nearest exit hatch.

A Callistan paced to and fro close by it, on guard.

Jarl waited till the creature turned, then leaped and dubbed it down with the barrel of his ray gun. In seconds, he was spinning back the hatch-bolts.

The hatch swung wide, and night poured in...the blistering, dust-choked desert night, pale with the light reflected by looming Venus' unbroken mists and billowing cloudbanks.

Somewhere, out there, were primitives in hideous metal masks, so fierce that even the almighty Federation at last had forbidden this satellite to all men.

Perhaps, too, here were robots...towering metal monsters from beyond the stars, brought down by destiny in its strange workings to save the outlaw worlds.

Or perhaps not. Perhaps this seared and storm-swept ball held only the end of Wassreck's dreams...and death.

Jarl Corvett smiled a thin, wry smile. At least, he'd know the answer soon.

Breathing deep, he swung out through the hatch and dropped down on Womar...

CHAPTER EIGHT

MORNING on Womar. The hot winds were flames Whipping at Jarl's face, and the driven sand slashed and burned like pelting needles. Slowly, the night died and, off to his right, the sun rose-fiery, incandescent. Venus, to his left, stretched in a great, shining arc as far as the eye could see. Dust swirled about him in smothering clouds. He wallowed through a sea of powdery; ankle-deep grit where rocks shoved up in hidden reefs to trap him. Hollows loomed in his bloodshot eyes like chasms; and hillocks grew to mountains up which he toiled on hands and knees, choking and gasping. His cheeks were rasped raw now, his lips all parched and cracking.

Still he lurched onward—lost and disoriented, without destination.

But not without goal.

A goal—? He laughed aloud—the muddled, drunken laughter of a heat-twisted brain. Yes, he had a goal; but it was the goal of utter madness.

For somewhere in this blazing waste. Womar's primitives lay waiting. He knew; he'd seen them charge before. How they sensed an alien's coming was a secret no stranger had ever fathomed. But sense it they did; so they'd hide and wait, till at last the sun and dust and slashing wind had done their work and the invader fell and could not rise.

Then, and then only, they would come, from whatever dark, hidden maze they came from. Their blood-thirsting screams would rise above the howling wind, and their hideous metal masks would flash like mirrors of madness in the white flame of the sunlight.

And after that...Jarl choked on his parched, swelling tongue. After that, there would come other things...things no alien being had survived, rites so awful as to make this blazing wilderness seem a cool Elysium.

What was left, they'd spread out in neat display as their own black warning to other straying strangers.

That was his goal: that the primitives should seize him.

Yet now, as the moment neared when he would fall to rise no more, he knew of a sudden how mad it was. Not even Ceresta and the raider fleet were worth it; not even freedom. Nothing could be worth it.

But now, there was no turning back. He'd come too far; he'd pressed his luck one time too many.

Swaying and staggering, he came to another, deeper hollow, where bare rock showed through the dust and sand along the slopes in serrate ledges. At the bottom, the drifting grit lay in smooth-swept whorls like a hill-bounded cove where ripples had somehow been trapped in motion, frozen into the surface of the water.

He laughed once, wildly, and lurched ahead; then slipped and pitched forward, tumbling headlong. Rocks gashed at him as he fell—tearing, clutching, as if even they shared the primitives' hatred for all aliens.

Stunned, choked, half blinded, he came to rest at last at the edge of the pool of rippled sand. Here, away from the sweep of the wind, the heat bore down like a smothering blanket. Jarl's brain reeled. He could draw no strength from the air that scorched his lungs. He knew instinctively that no being of his race could long survive the drain and pressure.

Frantically, he dragged himself up and wallowed forward, out onto the sand.

Even as his feet sank into the sifting dust, he knew he should have gone the other way, back up the slope. But by then it was too late. Deeper he sank, and deeper, till the loose sand was thigh-high about his legs.

DESPERATELY, he threw himself flat, trying to spread the weight of his body. But the grit gave way beneath him, sliding and swirling, hungrily sucking him deeper. Dust clogged his nostrils. When he tried to open his mouth to suck air, sand flooded in.

He floundered wildly, and the thought flashed through his mind, *Do I die here—here, in this whirlpool of shifting grit, swallowed up, buried alive, before I even find the primitives...?*

He struggled again to rise, and could not. The choking dust swirled higher. His senses dimmed. The blazing sun began to darken.

And then they came.

They came with a rush, across the crest, their metal masks blurred to blinding flashes. Out of the clefts of the rocks they came, and up from the sand-pool's edges, howling like the screaming's in a nightmare, the wailings of banshees.

Their bodies were brown as the sun-blistered rocks, their shoulder-plumes scarlet as heart-blood. Their girdles were scarlet, too, and the plumed bands that circled wrists and ankles. Monstrous footgear, broad as their lean, hard bodies, sprayed sand as they charged. Light flared in iridescent splendor from strange, outré weapons.

Desperately, Jarl tried again to rise. But again, the eddying grit gave way beneath him.

Then they were upon him—seizing him, dragging him up and out of the powder-dry morass that held him. The great webbed shoes they wore did not sink in, but, rather, skimmed the surface.

Vainly, Jarl struck out and sought to struggle. But he was as a child in the grip of giants. The primitives' hands were like shackling bands of steel upon him.

He let himself go limp. After all, was this not the very thing he'd come for?

Unless they killed him here and now...

But they carried him back bodily to the sand-pool's edge, to a place where the serrate rocks rose in lowering, brooding ledges. A crevice yawned. Swiftly, they shoved him between the saw-toothed boulders, down into it.

Now other hands reached up from the depths of an inner cavern to receive him. He found himself lifted into the black emptiness of a narrow tunnel.

Then he was on his own feet once more. But the hands still gripped, his arms, pushing him along as he stumbled through the ebon passage. Dimly, he became aware of a strange odor in his nostrils—a sweet yet musty scent he'd never smelled before.

THE passage led on, ever downward. Steadily it grew cooler. Jarl began to lose the sense of draining pressure. His captors jabbered in the darkness. But their speech was like no tongue he'd ever heard before, all consonants and gutturals.

It seemed they hurried on for miles. Then, at last, a dim light showed ahead.

The party halted. Someone clamped a heavy metal mask upon Jarl's head—a mask with neither eye nor ear-holes. It shut him off in a throbbing private night, through which the guttural voices drifted only as dim whispers.

Once more, the primitives shoved Jarl ahead, and as they moved forward, he had a sudden feeling that they had left the tunnel and come out into a larger room.

Then they were lifting him again; laying him down flat on some smooth surface; holding him there, rigid.

He clenched his teeth, bracing himself for the torture that he knew would sooner or later be his lot.

But no pain came. Instead, of a sudden, the surface on which he lay was vibrating, moving. Air whipped at him. With a shock, he realized that he and the others were hurtling through Womar's heart at jarring speed on some strange transport unit.

It made his spine crawl, just a little. How primitive were these primitives? Had all the worlds been wrong about them? What dark secrets did they hold hidden, here in these black caves that honeycombed the rock beneath this satellite's blazing deserts?

And what of the robots? Where were they hidden?

Or did they exist at all—?

But he had no time to ponder, for as suddenly as the motion had begun, it ended. The rush of air slowed, then halted. Once more, the primitives' hands were lifting him, dragging him forward.

But this time the passageway through which they moved led upward.

The heat rose as they climbed, till Jarl was sweating and choking inside the helmet. Then the slope leveled off again, and he sensed that they had come out into another, larger room. New voices joined the dim whisperings of his escort, till their volume swelled to a tremendous, throbbing chorus. Bodies buffeted against Jarl, milling about him. Hands clawed at him— clubbing, tugging, scratching. He could feel the crowd's hot hate crushing in upon him. The musty, cloying, sweetish odor he'd smelled before grew even stronger till he was sick and dizzy, ready to vomit.

His captors pressed on, not hesitating. Roughly, they led Jarl stumbling up a flight of steps.

At the top, there was a brief halt.

Then the faint squeal of massive hinges.

A blast of heat struck Jarl a hammer blow. He reeled under its impact.

From behind, someone gave him a savage shove. He lurched forward.

A new burst of sound smashed at him, even through the metal helmet—a wild shout, torn from a thousand throats, fierce and welling in its hatred. The heat and smell were great sledges, pounding at him.

IN spite of all of his control, Jarl felt a sudden rush of panic. Stumbling, staggering, he came upright—fists clenched, braced to meet the fury of those about him even in his helplessness, his blindness.

But again hands seized him before he could strike a blow. Someone fumbled at the catches of the shrouding helmet.

The metal mask came away. Sound, light, heat, stench, smashed in on Jarl.

He jerked back and threw his hands up across his eyes, trying to shut out the blinding blaze of Womar's sun.

But other hands jerked down his own. Blinking, half blinded, stiff with shock, he stared out incredulously upon a sight such as he had never seen before.

For he stood in the prow of a great space ship—a ship vast beyond the belief of mortal man.

It was old, this ship—old with an age that staggered Jarl Corvett's mind. Eons were in the sagging plates and splitting arches. The crystals that glinted in the dull, warped metal spoke of untold ages here on Womar. The hull was smashed and shattered, too, and the blazing sun poured in through a thousand great jagged holes and rifts. One whole end of the craft was crumpled, buckled, where it had plowed deep into the rocks and sand as it crashed here.

And it was alien. A thousand differences stood out in line and structure and material. The size alone would have been enough to mark it as having come from outside this solar system. Yet without bulkheads, without bracing, the mass of it loomed as one incredibly vast and far-spreading room—an engineering feat to stagger man's imagination.

And here, too, were the primitives, heirs to Womar's scorched, windswept deserts. A thousand strong—ten thousand—they packed the huge hold in a screaming, seething mass, metal masks hideously aglint in the streaming sunlight.

But for Jarl Corvett, ship and primitives alike were mere incidentals. Swaying, staring, he could find eyes only for one thing: the robots.

The robots—! He rocked—incredulous, unbelieving.

But here they were—metal monsters that towered rank on rank in this great hold, like monstrous originals of the figures in *Ktar* Wassreck's workshop. Like a forest they rose...a forest of utter, malign menace.

Their feet alone stood higher than a tall man's head; and the glinting orientation-slots of the great head-units towered so far above the crowd as to have been beacon lights on distant mountains.

Chill, unmoving, they stood here in the hull of this shattered ship as they had stood for ages. But where ship and fittings were decaying, these mighty warriors still shone resplendent, fabricated of some different, finer metal. Strength gleamed in every line of their orange-gold figures. The screaming primitives were only ants that crawled and danced and raged upon them.

STARING at them, Jarl Corvett could only choke and tremble. There was room for but one thought within his reeling brain: *Wassreck was right—! He was right! He was right...!*

It made this whole mad gamble worth the while. Even if he died here, all his efforts unavailing, it would still be worth it.

And what could not an army of these giant automatons accomplish? What chance would even the mighty Federation stand against them?

It was destiny. More surely even than he knew his name, Jarl knew that destiny had brought him here...the strange, dark destiny of courage and fighting men that ever seemed to ride on the side of the outlaw worlds, and freedom.

But now that he was here, destiny would need a strong right arm to implement it.

His arm.

He swung round, then, with his old, bold coat of arrogance upon him—surveying his captors, searching for some faintest hint of hidden weakness.

But the primitives did not waver. Their eyes stayed cold, leering out at him from their metal masks, grim as the day of judgment.

Those masks... With a sudden rush of recognition, it came to Jarl that their stylized patterns were modeled after the head-units of the towering robots.

Such a little thing, that recognition. Yet again, Jarl felt his tension lift a fraction. He smiled a thin, wry smile and waited.

But now, to one side of the stage-like platform on which he and his escort party stood, there was a sudden stir of motion. A new door opened in what had been a bulkhead barring the way to another part of the ancient, fallen ship.

A cry went up from the seething multitude. The mass of primitives surged forward, close against the platform.

Slowly, creaking and groaning, a great stone slab was wheeled forth. Its sides were deep-graven with carved figures...strange, hideous figures that writhed in ecstasy and anguish. Stains smudged its upper surface. Heavy metal clamps, long age-corroded, were set into each corner.

With a sickening jolt, it came to Jarl that it was an altar.

Straining and grunting, a crew of primitives tugged it into position in the platform's center.

Jarl's captors gripped his arms.

The panting group by the altar straightened and hurried back through the door in the bulkhead. Rattling sounds came forth. A moment later, the primitives reappeared, rolling out a monstrous, shining metal tub on wheels, big as one of the kettledrums of the spider men of Rhea. Its sides were graven with the same contorted figures as the altar.

The din of the crowd swelled louder. Masked primitives leaped and screamed in impassioned frenzy.

Tight-jawed, Jarl waited.

The wheeled tub was set in place beside the altar. It moved easily and smoothly. Then, again, the altar crew retreated through the bulkhead.

This time, when they returned, they bore a living, struggling creature.

MAN-SIZED, the thing was like no animal Jarl had ever seen before, with brown, bead-like skin and tiny brain case. Off-hand, he judged it to belong to some desert species native to this grit-drifted hellhole, Womar.

The primitives carried it to the altar; clamped its spraddled body face up atop the stone with the ancient shackles. The din of the crowd was deafening.

Somewhere on high, a great gong sounded. The shouts and screaming died away.

In the same instant, a new door opened in the bulkhead. Another primitive stepped forth; paused, posing.

This creature's garb was different from the others! His metal mask was ebon. So were his plumes, his girdle. A great scarlet jewel was set in the forehead of the dead-black helmet. His hands were gloved in sleek jet gauntlets.

Now, while Jarl watched, the posing primitive's arms came up, till the gloved hands were high above his head, displayed, as if they were a symbol.

The throng below stood frozen, rigid.

The black-masked primitive strode forward, to a spot between the altar and the shining metal tub. Swiftly, he lifted the lid that capped the drum-like vat.

Two of the altar-crew rushed forward and held it open for him. Another held out a strange implement that, to Jarl, looked like some crude sort of grease gun.

The black-masked figure dipped the nozzle of the thing into the tub and worked a plunger, then turned to the struggling life form shackled to the altar. Deftly, he stabbed the snout of the tool into a spot below the creature's breastbone.

The captive tried to jerk away, to no avail. With smooth precision, the primitive in black pressed home the plunger.

A gusty sigh ran through the throng about the platform. It came to Jarl that he was cold as ice despite the heat and blazing sun. The musty, sweetish smell he'd caught before swirled about him, even stronger.

The black-masked figure straightened. With quick, sure movements, he twisted at a fitting, then lifted away the tool. The nozzle he left sticking in the creature on the altar. It thrust up from the hollow below the breastbone like the hilt of a deep-plunged dagger.

The two primitives by the wheeled tub let the lid fall back. Turning, one darted to the bulkhead door. When he came out, he bore a flaring torch.

New silence fell upon the crowd, so complete that the altar crewman's footsteps rang and echoed in the stillness.

He passed the torch to his black-masked fellow.

Black-Mask swung the flaming brand on high and, turning, faced Jarl Corvett. His voice thundered, harsh and guttural.

Jarl stood rock-rigid. The words he could not understand. But the threat, the menace—they needed no translator.

PIVOTING, the primitive stepped back from the altar; thrust out the torch till its flame touched the tip of the nozzle protruding out of the shackled prisoner's chest.

Of a sudden Jarl's whole body was drenched with icy sweat. He could not move; he could not breathe. The tales of horror he'd heard so many times swirled through his brain.

For an instant, nothing happened.

Then, all at once, there was a puff of sound, a flash of flame above the captive. A great black jet of smoke shot high into the air, out of the nozzle.

The life form on the altar gave one shrill cry that was agony, incarnate. Its body jerked and twisted, lashing against the shackles in a frenzy.

The primitives went mad. The huge room rocked with their howls and screamings.

But Jarl Corvett hardly heard them.

He'd seen cruel death before, on a dozen far-flung planets.

But this...

For while he watched, thin lines of fire were racing along the doomed sacrifice's writhing body. In a spreading network, the flesh itself was bursting open, flames leaping up in a thousand places.

In a searing flash, the truth came to Jarl: *The creature's blood was burning!*

He sagged in his escort's grip, and retched—shock-stunned, sick with horror.

But the primitives who flanked him jerked him upright. An open hand stung his face with brutal slaps.

The spell that gripped Jarl broke. Numb, tight-jawed, he forced himself to look again upon the altar.

The shackled creature lay there still, a charred, contorted horror.

While Jarl watched, the monster in the ebon mask stepped back and passed the torch to the altar crewman who had brought it. Other primitives undamped the gyves and dragged the corpse away.

Again Black-Mask brought up his hands. Again the crowd's tumultuous hubbub faded.

Black-Mask's hands came down. He swung about till he faced Jarl. Imperiously, he gestured.

Jarl's captors dragged him forward. The torchbearer stepped quickly back, out of their path.

Fear was in Jarl Corvett, then—a fear that verged on shrieking terror. His body seemed like a thing apart—a statue carved from living ice, with no relation to his being.

But hate came with the terror, a flaming hate that grew at every step, till its white-hot fire ate, up the fear and burned away his sickness and his trembling. Of a sudden he was himself again. He sucked in air. Without volition, his muscles stiffened against the digging fingers of his savage escort.

They jerked him up short before the altar. The black-masked figure shook a jet-gloved fist and shouted guttural imprecations.

THE last shreds of Jarl's terror vanished, washed away in the flood of his tormentor's fury. Out of nowhere, a thing that Wassreck once had said came flashing to him: *Hate is the face of fear, not courage.*

That hate which showed in the primitive's every line and gesture—it, too, was born of terror...a welling fear of all and any beings who came down from the skies to Womar.

Jarl laughed aloud, it was so funny—that he and this other should face each other so, in deadly menace, when within they were only quivering twins of terror.

And as he laughed, his own hate died the same swift death to which his fear had fallen. A grim, bleak poise replaced them both. For if the primitives, in their hearts, felt the self-same few that he had, there was still a chance for recklessness to blaze a path through this wilderness of desperation.

His laugh cut short the black-masked figure's shouting. The primitive stared at him, as if unbelieving.

Cold-eyed, cold-nerved, Jarl drew himself to his full height. Rigid, he probed for some—for any—last wild gambit.

But Black-Mask, too, was straightening. He cried out fiercely to his helpers.

They shoved Jarl forward.

As they did so, the primitive beside the huge, wheeled tank lifted up the lid.

Jarl glanced down into it.

The vat was full. The awful broth almost lapped the brim. From it, in sickening waves, rose the sweetish, cloying fumes Jarl had come to associate with the primitives.

Black-Mask leaned forward. Shouting again, he lashed out. His jet-gloved fist raked at Jarl's face.

Instinctively, Jarl rocked back. New tides of black despair washed through him. What could he do, locked in his captor's grasp, hemmed between tank and torch-bearer, black-masked fiend and blood-drenched altar?

Tank—and torchbearer—!

That link…in an instant it grew to a searing, surging flame, hotter even than these creatures' own hell-fire brew.

Spasmodically, Jarl twisted round.

The primitive with the blazing brand still stood statue-like at the corner of the great stone slab.

Black-Mask snarled another order. His henchmen jerked Jarl back—lifting him, swinging him upward, till he hung suspended above the altar.

By instinct, Jarl wrenched against them; felt them, too, stiffen in the face of his resistance.

But if he could not fight them, perhaps there was another way…

Before they could lower him to the slab, he let himself go limp, loose-limbed and unresisting as any corpse.

It broke their balance. He hit the stone with a sodden thud…lay there unmoving, head lolled back.

For the fraction of a second their grip relaxed.

IT was Jarl's moment… Savagely, then, he lashed out with all his might, in a violent spasm of arms and legs and torso. His feet smashed the metal mask into one primitive's face. His elbow sank fist-deep in another's midriff.

The restraining hands fell from him.

Desperately, he threw himself across the altar, toward the torchbearer. Before the creature could recoil, Jarl was upon him—smashing him down with fists and knees and shoulders; snatching the flaming brand out of his hands.

Falling over each other in their haste, the others lunged to seize Jarl.

But instead of fleeing, he leaped back onto the altar. There was a prayer in his heart—his heart in his mouth. With a wild curse, he hurled the torch straight for the vat of hell-broth.

It struck the open lid, then plunged on down into the liquid.

But even as it fell, the fumes were flaring. Flame and smoke leaped up in a roaring column. A cloudburst of liquid fire sprayed out in all directions.

The cries of the primitives exploded into one great scream of pain and terror. As Jarl threw himself flat, with the altar-stone between him and the tank, he glimpsed the reeling, flame-cased figure of his jet-masked tormentor—stumbling, falling.

Then the black smoke billowed out in nauseous, all-obscuring murk that swallowed even the thundering holocaust that still roared around what had been the tank of liquid.

Jarl rolled from the wheeled platform on which the altar rested. Bent double, he raced through the choking haze for the bulkhead. In seconds, he was fumbling his way along it to the nearest doorway…slipping through and ramming the heavy bolt home behind him.

Ahead, a shaft and spiral stairway loomed. Panting, he sprinted upward, past level after level.

The stairway ended against another metal door.

The outlined figure of one of the mighty warrior robots was blazoned on it.

Jarl's heart pounded harder.

Shoving open the hatch, he half-fell inside and locked it, too, behind him.

He found himself now in a control room. Panels thick with dust lined three of its walls. The fourth was a single massive, transparent, plastic plate through which occupants could look out across the great hold where the robots were massed…where brief moments before Jarl Corvett had stood face to face with hideous death.

Stumbling to it, Jarl stared down upon the smoke-smirched scene below. Flames still were leaping about the platform.

Here and there, he could catch dim glimpses of primitives' hurrying figures as they ran among the metal monsters.

OVERHEAD, the dense black smoke almost hid the roof. Eddying, slowly rising, it swirled out through the cracks and rifts in the ancient hull, up into the blazing, sunlit heat of Womar's desert sky.

Of a sudden Jarl was weak to the point of sickness. Numbly, he turned and surveyed the rest of the control room with a closer scrutiny.

Bank after bank of dials and indicators marked with strange symbols leered down at him like a host of huge blank eyes. Against the far wall, units with focussing plates like the viziscreens of his own solar system were ranged in a precise row.

And everywhere—on every panel, every instrument—were stamped neat, stylized images of the warrior robots.

The numbness in Jarl grew. He knew instinctively, without question, that this was the place sought by *Ktar* Wassreck—the brain, the nerve center, for the shining metal monsters that were to have saved the warrior worlds.

But now that he was here, what could he do? His own ignorance was a tight-drawn, all-concealing blindfold.

With time enough, and skill and patience, he might perhaps have worked his way through to an understanding of how the robots were controlled. But time was the one thing he did not have. Second by second, the precious hours were ticking by. As far as he was concerned—lacking knowledge, training, understanding—he might as well have been on Venus.

And so the warrior worlds would die. The Federation fleet would sweep down on Ceresta.

Already, the three days given by *rey* Gundre were running out...

Jarl shook in the grip of helpless, frustrating fury. He had come so far; yet now that he was here, he could do nothing.

He cursed aloud; and as he did so, a new sound drifted to him.

A familiar sound...the sound of a space ship's blasting rockets.

He whirled; leaped back to the broad expanse of transparent plastic panel.

He reached it just in time to see a great section in the top of the hull above the hold suddenly buckle and crash down. Sunlight streamed through smoke and dust.

The roar of the blasting rockets echoed louder. A moment later, another huge chunk of hull tore loose and fell. Then another, and another, till the hole showed like a spreading canopy of sky above the robots.

Below, the last of the primitives were fleeing. Breathing hard, pressed tight to the observation panel, Jarl watched and waited.

The rocket-roar took on the peculiar whistling sound that went with ramping. Before Jarl's eyes, a ship dropped down stern-first into the hold and rocked to a landing amid the debris and towering robots.

Now the ship, as well as the sound, was suddenly familiar.

Too familiar.

It was the flagship of High Commissioner *rey* Gundre's mighty Federation fleet!

CHAPTER NINE

JARL Corvett lay flat on his belly on the floor of the room that housed the brain of the warrior robots, staring bleakly down into the hold below.

Then, again, he twisted, shifted. This endless waiting—it was enough to drive a saint to murder.

How long had it been—two hours—or two eons?

It was a time for thinking—because there was nothing else to do but think. Escape was not even a thing to dream about by daylight, with primitives still roving through these warrens. Tonight, perhaps, a man might find a way; but for now there was only...thinking.

So Jarl lay there on the floor, sweating and shifting. Narrow-eyed, he studied the motionless bulk that was the flagship, and asked himself a thousand questions.

Questions he could not answer.

Why would *rey* Gundre, of all the players in this mad drama, come roaring down on Womar? What did he seek? How had he found his way here?

Above all, what was he waiting for this way—jets dead and hatches still unopened?

And for him to pick the robot-hold of this ancient ship to land in...

Unless, by some wild chance, *Ktar* Wassreck had escaped—

Even the thought made Jarl's heart leap.

But then it quieted down again, drained by the dark, dull hopelessness within him.

The time for dreams was dead and gone. For all his bravado and boasting he, Jarl Corvett, had failed the man who'd come for him on Horla. By now, at best, *Ktar* Wassreck lay a corpse in the chill horror of Venus' *slan*-chambers.

Pain welled up in Jarl, and with it came new sickness. Choking, he buried his face against his arms and cursed the day his mother bore him.

But his mind would not stay still. Drearily, he thought about the others.

About Ungo and Ylana, Bor Legat, Sais...

It only brought new anguish. For he'd failed them, too; failed them one and all...Ungo, friend of friends, who'd trusted him beyond, all others...Ylana, vision of golden loveliness—betraying her world and, her own father just to save him...Bor Legat of Mercury, murderous and merciless, yet loyal in his twisted way to the raider cause.

And Sais.

Dark Sais, *Ktar* Wassreck's daughter. Even in this place, Jarl could recapture the fragrance of her hair, the pulsing pressure of her perfect body. She was all woman...

And all Jarl Corvett's.

So he'd brought her down to this wild world and left her to the mercies of Tas Karrel's raider rabble.

Cursing again, he writhed about and once more stared up at the banks of panels.

But that was all that he could do. He did not even dare to rise and experiment with the controls spread out before him, for fear someone below would glimpse the movement.

Then, from the hold, there rose a sudden clatter.

Jarl swung back to the plastic window, craning and peering.

BELOW, the main hatch of *rey* Gundre's ship was opening. Blue-uniformed Federation crewmen poured out, weapons glinting, and took up positions amid the debris.

In the same instant, the high whine of a light, fast-traveling carrier cut through the hold.

A moment later, a slim, swift craft dropped through the gaping hole in the ancient hull and set down for a landing.

Its prow was marked with Bor Legat's black lightning-flash insignia.

Incredulously, Jarl dug his nails into the plastic.

The carrier came to rest. Its hatch swung open. A burly *dau* leaped out.

Instantly, the Federation crewmen came to their feet and crowded round.

But the *dau* ignored them. Turning, he gestured to someone still inside the carrier.

Another figure dropped down...a figure with shimmering golden hair and a scarlet tunic that emphasized the slim, ripening womanhood of the one who wore it.

Ylana—!

Jarl caught his breath. His palms were suddenly slick with sweat, the muscles of his chest constricted.

While he, watched, the girl moved calmly to the Federation flagship.

The *dau* swung back aboard the carrier. The hatch clanged shut. A moment later, the craft was in the air again, lancing out of the ancient hull and away.

Ylana disappeared into the flagship.

Jarl sank back, trembling. Brow furrowed, lips dry, he tried to make sense of this new maneuver.

It was plain now what had happened to the girl, and Ungo. Bor Legat had captured them that night, back on Ceresta. Now he was carrying out his plan to trade her life for time, and the desperate chance that somehow Ceresta might be defended.

But why should he meet *rey* Gundre here? What had led the two of them to choose this shattered hulk for their rendezvous?

Jarl looked down once more.

More crewmen were hurrying from the flagship—clearing the debris from around the ramping-spot; setting up a perimeter studded with heavy weapons.

They planned to stay a while; that much was plain.

But why? Why, why *why—?*

The question rang in Jarl's brain like a tolling bell. But he still could find no answer.

Another hour dragged by. Slowly, the shadows of ship and robots lengthened. Hunger gnawed at Jarl's belly. He moved this way and that, trying to work the ache from his weary muscles.

DOWN in the hold, the crewmen moved more slowly. Yet even up here, high above them, Jarl could sense a rising tension. It showed in the way they kept looking towards the burrows into which the primitives had fled...their sudden starts, their readiness with their weapons.

He hunched forward, narrow-eyed, resting his weight upon his elbows.

Then there was a flurry about the hatch as a Thorian officer barked orders. The crewmen snapped to smart attention.

A moment later *rey* Gundre himself strode down the ramp, a lean, imposing figure. Ylana followed, close behind him.

Together, they moved about the perimeter's defenses, then started back towards the great ship's hatchway.

But now Ylana hesitated, and there was a brief moment of discussion. The golden hair rippled as she shook her head and gestured.

Her father's shoulders lifted in a shrug. Pivoting, he went on up the ramp without her.

Ylana turned. Almost aimlessly, she wandered out among the robots; paused and leaned back against a gigantic metal foot, watching the blue-uniformed crewmen as they toiled and sweated.

The shadows grew longer. The crewmen ceased to heed her presence.

She moved, then, swiftly, silent as the deepening dusk— sliding around the foot in one quick motion; darting past an unmanned post of the perimeter defenses to a spot out of view amid the tangled debris.

Jarl went rigid. Twisting, he worked his way along the observation plate to a place where he again could see her.

But already she was on the move again, creeping on hands and knees, farther and farther from the flagship.

Where was she going? Why had she broken out of the circle?

And what if the primitives should catch her?

The thought brought Jarl to his feet, shuddering.

Besides, with the thickening gloom down in the hold, perhaps this time he could get an answer to his questions.

With one last glance to chart the course that the girl might follow, he ran to the door and threw back the bolt; then slid out and felt his way down the black well that was the spiral stairway.

In seconds he was at the bulkhead door. Opening it a crack, he weighed his chances.

The crewmen still were busy with their tasks inside the network of defenses. The pools of shadow hung all enshrouding. Flat on his belly, he wriggled forth and crept along the wall in the same direction he'd seen Ylana take.

Out here, once more he caught the cloying, sweetish scent of the hell-broth, mixed with smoke, and the knot in his belly tightened. The shadows loomed like grim reminders of the primitives' dark fury.

He moved faster.

BACK around the ship, a ring of blinding lights came on, as if to emphasize the death that lurked in the outer darkness. Jarl surged to his feet. Stiff with tension, he searched the gloom for some hint of Ylana.

Off to the right, close by the bulkhead, a dull sound rang, as of some object striking metal.

Groping, Jarl found a breaker brace-bar to serve him as a weapon. Wary, taut-nerved, he worked his way towards the spot from which the noise had come.

But he found nothing. Grim recognition of the hopelessness of his task crept through him.

He fought it down. Swinging round, deliberately, he kicked a crystallizing metal plate fallen from the great hull's roof.

The sound echoed, loud and startling in the silence. Jarl stood stock-still, straining his ears for some reaction.

So close at hand it made him jerk, there was a sudden rasp of movement.

Heedless now of noise, Jarl sprinted towards it. In a mighty leap, he cleared a heap of black-scorched litter.

Ylana crouched beyond it. Face a white blotch in the murk, she started up as he made the hurdle. Her mouth came open. He could hear the first whisper of a scream rising in her throat.

Savagely, he jammed his open palm across her mouth and swept her to him, smothering her kicks and blows and struggles. Lips close to her ear, he rasped, "Ylana! It's me—Jarl..."

He could feel her muscles contract, her body stiffen. Then, suddenly, she was limp in his arms—clinging to him, half-sobbing.

"Quick! We've got to move!" He dragged her with him, on along the bulkhead, then off amid the black mass of the debris.

Halting, finally, once more he strained his ears, listening for any hint that they'd been heard and followed.

But none came. At last, relaxing, he let go of her and slumped down into the drifted sand and litter.

He could feel the girl's eyes on him. But he held his silence.

"Jarl Corvett..." she choked. And then, in a rush: "Thank the Gods you came, Jarl; so glad..."

She dropped down close beside him, her shoulder pressing against him, her hand on his.

Turning, he studied her.

The grey eyes were black-shadowed, her lovely face deep-lined.

Of a sudden he wanted nothing so much as to embrace her.

But there were so many questions to be answered...

He flung them at her bluntly: "Why did they come here, Ylana—your father; Bor Legat? What brought them down to Womar—to this ship?"

He could see her soft lips quiver. For an instant the grey eyes wavered.

BUT then they raised again and met his gaze. She said: "My father is a traitor, Jarl Corvett—a traitor to himself and all the things he believes in, and to the Federation."

Jarl stared, unspeaking.

The girl's mouth worked. Her fingers gouged his hand.

Jarl—oh Jarl..." Agony was in her voice. "Before: I told you how he'd loot Ceresta. Now—now he's gone the whole way. He dreams of still more power—of carving out an empire, destroying the Federation with its own fleet. His orders—I learned today they were to arrange a truce and spare Ceresta, give the asteroids their freedom and bring them into the Federation on even terms. But he's beyond that. All he can think of is loot and power, destruction. He's mad—mad, Jarl; stark, raving mad."

The girl's voice broke. Sobbing, she buried her face against Jarl's shoulder.

Hard-jawed, tight-lipped, he held her close. But he did not dare let feeling touch him. Not now, with time so short; so much at stake.

If the asteroids could hold their freedom, even in the Federation; if Ceresta and the raider fleet were only spared…

"And you—?" he clipped. "Where were you going? Why did you try to run away?"

Ylana lifted a tear-smudged face. All at once her chin was firm and her lips no longer trembled.

She said: "Once I would have betrayed him for you alone, Jarl Corvett. This time, I came to do it for the Federation—and for freedom."

"You mean—?"

Her laugh held bitterness and pain. "The fleet commanders do not know my father's orders. I thought to reach Bor Legat's ship and warn them."

"Then Legat—"

"He came here only to bring me to my father, in hopes that he could save Ceresta. He'd channel a message through his viziscreen."

Jarl's breath came faster. There was a pricking and tingling along his spine.

He let go of Ylana; surged to his feet.

The girl rose, slim and straight beside him. "Yes, Jarl—?"

Jarl laughed, deep in his throat. Suddenly hunger and fatigue and pain were nothing. He saw only his dreams, his goal. "I'll get to Legat, Ylana! By all the gods of the void, I swear it!"

Her words came, swift and eager: "And I'll go with you!"

"No, Ylana—"

"Yes!" Fists clenched, face tight with strain again, she stepped back from him. "I've earned the right, Jarl! You can't leave me!"

For a long, long moment, he looked deep into her eyes. There were so many things to see there—courage, and anguish; fierce loyalty, determination, pain.

She hurled words at him—commanding and entreating: "You'll need me, Jarl! You can't find Legat's ship without me. It's close—it and the Knife. We can reach them by the time it dawns, if we go together—"

Still Jarl stared into her eyes, unspeaking.

She broke off. Her hand came up, swept back the rippling golden hair. Her throat was a smooth-carved ivory column, her face a lovely mirror of the things that shone deep in her eyes.

SLOWLY, Jarl smiled. He knew there was no need for other answer. And words could be such futile, empty things.

Her hand in his, together they crept on through the debris; up through a broken port set high in the side of the ancient hull.

Then they were out at last, into the windswept wastes of Womar's deserts...stumbling on through the sand and rocks, mile after mile. They had no breath for talk, no time for resting. A pause might bring the primitives down upon them.

Jarl gripped his brace-bar club and prayed.

Then light came dimly, herald to another blazing desert day. But with it, too, rose the lance-sharp outlines of the prows of two great raider ships, ramped amid a wilderness of jutting crags.

Jarl's heart leaped. Quick jubilation surged within him. "Ylana—!"

The girl screamed.

Jarl whirled—club up, fists clenching. "What—?"

But again, there was no need for words, for the girl was pointing back across the endless, dust-deep waste through which they'd come to an ominous moving figure.

The figure of a mighty warrior robot, a metal giant that loomed like a monstrous, man-made nightmare against the clear blue of the morning sky.

Jarl rocked—incredulous, unbelieving. His club-arm sagged down to his side.

With every fleeting second, the metal monster towered still larger, closer. Its massive legs swung out in wallowing, league-long strides, closing the gap between them.

Ylana cried out again. She darted to Jarl; clung close against him, shaking like a slim reed in a wind.

He tore free from his shell of shock and frozen fascination. Sweeping the girl up, he raced for the nearest outcropping of jagged rock.

The giant from beyond the void stalked nearer. The clanking of the great joints rolled down on them like distant thunder.

Ylana sobbed, "My father—he must have found that I was gone—"

Jarl did not answer. Drawing her down behind the rocks, he waited, as for the Juggernaut of fate itself.

The monster thundered closer, great feet grinding stones to powder with every stride. The rising sun's rays transformed the mighty, gleaming torso to a living statue carved in orange-gold fire.

Ylana shook with a new wave of paroxysmal panic. It took every ounce of Jarl's control to hold himself from leaping up and running—tearing his heart apart in one last frantic, desperate flight.

But what good would it do to run, when this monstrous menace could overtake and pass him in a single stride?

Heart in his throat, he pulled Ylana close against him and waited in rigid, aching tension for his doom.

Another clanking step…another; and the robot towered above them, mountain-high.

JARL'S straining muscles cramped with pain. In awful fascination, he felt the robot's shadow fall across them; watched as a gigantic foot came down. The very ground shook. Dust spurted in a smothering cloud.

It was as if death, personified, looked down upon them.

And then, incredibly, the ponderous leg swung out again—swept over them, past them, and crashed to earth again beyond.

Another step. The shadow lifted.

Jarl raised his head; stared, still not believing.

But the robot was still moving on—on, through the bleak crags and the wastelands.

On, towards the place where the prows of the space ships stood out against the sky.

Straining his eyes, Jarl could see tiny figures running, the headlong rush of panic in their stride.

But the robot was striding faster. A roar of rockets echoed dimly.

As one, the Knife and Bor Legat's *Lightning* blasted up into the sky.

But already the robot was leaping, pivoting, with hideous, awkward grace that spoke of awful strength beyond man's feeble understanding. Great, gleaming metal hands shot out and seized the *Lightning* in mid-air. A lance of light blazed from the force-spot in the forehead and blasted the *Knife* to shattered fragments before it cleared the rocks.

And even as the light-beam struck, the mighty arms were levering. The *Lightning's* hull-beam cracked and splintered. The body parted in a spray of shattered shards and clawing, falling crewmen.

Then it was over. With savage force, the robot hurled the broken ship to the ground…trampled the shattered hull-sections into the dust.

Ylana clung to Jarl—choking, crying, whole body shaking. Tightlipped, holding her close, he pressed back against the rocks, so hard the ridges gouged his flesh like blunt-edged bayonets.

The metal giant was turning, now. Again its great feet clanged and thundered. Back it came once more, along the same road that had brought it to its terrible festival of carnage and destruction. Again, its shadow swept past Jarl and Ylana, not even pausing. Slowly, the thunder of its footsteps faded. The massive hulk grew smaller, smaller, in the distance.

Then it was gone. Heavily, Jarl Corvett struggled to his feet. Slowly, grimly, he turned.

Ylana's reddened eyes met his. "Jarl—! Where are you going?"

He shrugged; made himself ignore the new panic in her voice. "You can guess that, can't you?"

"No, Jarl! No—!" Eyes, wide, lips quivering and parted, she came up, clutching at his tunic.

He pushed her hands away, not daring to let the tenderness he felt show in face or action. His words came raw and harsh, in a voice he could hardly recognize as his own: "What else is there to do? The ships are gone. There's no other way that we can get in touch with Venus, fleet headquarters."

"No, Jarl…"

"But your father's got a ship." He bit his words off, clipped and hard. "He's got the robots, too, it seems—may the gods of the void protect us all! But if he should die…"

He let his voice trail off; stared out across the crags and desert wastes.

"Then I'll go, too—"

"No." He pushed her back again—grim, unrelenting. "A few of Bor Legat's men didn't get aboard the ship. Some may still live. Go stay with them till I come." And then, bleakly: *"If I come…"*

Turning without a backward glance, he plodded off through the scorching sand, following the course of the giant robot—

The course to *rey* Gundre and his flagship.

CHAPTER TEN

WOMAR'S blazing day—barely half as long as that of Earth—had waned again before Jarl reached his destination.

Then, at last, he was crawling through the dusk on hands and knees, up to the shattered hull of the ship from beyond the void. The sun had burned his face to a tortured mask, and his feet were raw, leaden lumps of flesh that left a trail of blood behind him.

Breathing hard, staggering weak from hunger and fatigue, he dragged himself up out of the dirt to the broken port. He did not even wonder what he would find within. He didn't care. He only knew that whatever he was to do, he must do quickly, before the last remnants of his draining strength were spent and he fell, to rise no more.

And what was he to do?

Drunkenly, he laughed. Who was he to say? His world was a blur of star-splotched black, and sometimes—too often—he saw stars that he knew weren't there. The time was past for schemes and planning.

At best, below, he'd die tonight.

But perhaps he might take *rey* Gundre with him.

rey Gundre, Ylana's father.

Her father—! No wonder her golden loveliness was shadowed. The real wonder was that madness hadn't claimed her.

But at least, this way, her sire's death would not be on her conscience. No one could claim that hers had been the hand to slay him.

DOWN in the hold, the Forspark lights were blazing. With a tremendous effort, Jarl pulled himself through the port. Half-sliding, half-falling, he skidded down into the dirt and debris; lay there for a moment, resting, dizzy and straining for breath to fill his lungs.

Then, lurching to his feet, he stared across at the ring of light; the flagship, ramped amid the forest of towering robots.

What turned a man like *rey* Gundre from the call of duty? Where did it start, that insatiate lust for power and booty?

And how, so quickly, had the high commissioner learned the secret of controlling the metal giants?

Had *Ktar* Wassreck talked before he died? Could he have sought to buy his life, at the last, with this final, priceless treasure?

But now, to think took too much effort. Now—Jarl swayed—he only knew that he must kill…that such power as this was too great to be trusted to any man, be he of the Federation or the raiders.

Yet how to reach him, there in the ship, while armed crewmen paced to and fro in the ring of light, on guard against the primitives?

The primitives…

Jarl leaned against the hull, and laughed his drunken laugh again.

The primitives: they held the answer.

Shuffling and stumbling, he worked his way through the piles of debris to the charred ruins of the altar platform. On hands and knees, he searched the tromped sand, probing amid the stinking litter.

Then, at last, his fingers touched the scorched, stiff corpse of a dead primitive, still sprawled in the dirt where the creature had fallen. Fumbling, he stripped off his own garments; replaced them with the corpse's shoulder-plumes and girdle, ankle and wristbands, sandals. Unclamping the hideous metal mask, he clamped it on his own head…smeared his body thick with sand and ashes.

Then it was done and he was ready, save for a weapon.

A weapon… He frowned. What weapon was there that he could carry past the guards who paced their posts about *rey* Gundre's ship?

Wearily, he sagged back on his haunches and let sand trickle through his fingers while he tried to prod his aching brain to action.

The grit piled up in a little heap between his knees, a dusty cone symbolic of this whole thrice-cursed desert world of Womar. It was everywhere, that grit and dust, underfoot and in the air alike. It rasped and smothered, choked and blinded.

And—it came to him in a sudden flash—it was the weapon he was seeking!

Scooping up the sand, he stuffed it between the girdle and his belly in sifting handfuls, till he could pack in no more.

And as he did so, his weariness fell away a little. A tiny spark of his old fire came alive again. A thread of the strength he'd thought was gone flowed slowly through him.

He found that he could even stand straight without staggering.

Bleakly, he laughed.

Then, breathing deep, throwing back his head, he howled the wild, harsh howl the charging primitives had uttered—pushed it out with all the volume he could muster.

He could see the guards jerk, in the light-ring round the ship. A ray gun blazed.

JARL crouched behind a pile of debris. After a moment, when the guards' first excitement had subsided, he moved in closer; howled again.

This time, the crewmen showed less tension. Grim, purposeful, they crouched by their weapons, watching and waiting.

Jarl moved still closer. He shouted—a guttural, clacking diatribe that went on for half a minute.

Two officers came to the nearest point of the defense perimeter. Uncertainly, they peered out into the echoing sea of darkness.

Again Jarl shouted; kept up the stream of clacking sound still longer.

One of the officers stepped back; gestured. A Forspark light swung round and focused on the area where Jarl lay hidden.

Jarl scraped his palms against his legs. Drum-like, his heart pounded. His belly writhed as he weighed the odds against this madman's gamble.

But there was no other way.

Once more he shouted; kept the clatter running.

And as he did so—slowly; open hands upthrust and empty—he rose to full height. Still shouting, he moved step by step into the beam of searching light.

He was close to the perimeter, now—close enough to hear the guards' excited babble.

Still no shot came; no ray-beam lanced out to burn him down.

Boldly, he strode forward, straight towards the defenses.

Crewmen moved up to meet him—cold-eyed, weapons leveled.

He reached the edge of the perimeter; stood there, waiting.

A *Fantay* officer came out. Ray gun in hand, throat-sac aquiver, he circled Jarl, uncertainty and puzzlement written on his ugly face.

Jarl threw out more of the meaningless, clacking syllables. The mask distorted them even further. They came out a guttural rattle like nothing ever heard on any planet.

A *Pervod* said, "Better take him in to the commissioner. Maybe the vocodor can make something of his gabble."

The *Fantay* nodded briefly. His pad-like hands moved over Jarl, probing the plumes, the wristbands, the girdle.

A trickle of sand spilled to the ground.

The *Fantay* brushed it off, unheeding. He reached up; started to fumble at the catches of the metal mask.

Jarl's heart leaped. He knocked away the officer's hand and hurled an angry cascade of gutturals at the creature.

The *Fantay* fell back a step, startled and even more uncertain; and an Earthman clipped, "Leave that tin hat alone, Beyno! This thing's a primitive. Maybe he thinks it's bad luck or something to take off his mask in front of strangers."

"Yes; that could be it." The officer swung around. "Gundre will be up in the control section. Let's take this *chitza* there."

TAKING Jarl's arm, he led him forward, centered amid the little knot of crewmen. Across the spreading ring of light they moved, and up the ramp into *rey* Gundre's mighty flagship…through echoing corridors…in and out of a lift that whisked them a dozen levels higher in as many seconds…down still another gleaming metal passage, till at last they faced the door of the craft's control section.

The officer let go of Jarl and stepped forward; touched the signal button.

The intercom plate glowed. *rey* Gundre's voice blared: "Yes! What is it?" He sounded tense and angry.

The *Fantay* clipped, "Sir, we've got one of the primitives. He came in of his own free will, but we can't understand what he's trying to say. We thought maybe you'd want to put him on the vocodor."

"A primitive—!" There was a moment's hesitation. Then: "All right. Just a minute."

The intercom plate went blank.

Jarl's knees were suddenly weak again. He swayed a little. Already, so soon, he was here. It had been incredibly simple.

But the next step—

Abruptly, the door to the control section opened part way. The high commissioner himself looked out. His lean, handsome face was haggard, the dark hair so rumpled that the white blaze was almost lost.

His deep-set eyes flicked to Jarl Corvett. Then he snapped, "Two guards will be enough," and drew back a fraction to let them enter.

They filed in—first the *Fantay* officer, then Jarl. The guards brought up the rear.

Behind them, *rey* Gundre closed and locked the door.

It was a bare, bleak room—the navigation unit, with its globes and astrocharts and viziscreens. Through a half-open door to the right, Jarl could see the switches and dial-studded panels of the operating cubicle; the empty pilot-chair.

Tight-drawn as a *llorin's* bowstring, he shifted, seeking the spot best suited to his purpose. Wry, mocking words *Ktar* Wassreck once had spoken rang in his brain: *"You'll live longer if you pick a place to run to before you have to run."*

Even now, as he faced certain death, it was good advice. Disregarding the others, he moved almost to the cubicle's doorway.

For the first time, then, as he swung round to face his captors, he saw the plate of the long-range viziscreen.

Saw it...rocked...almost cried out.

For there, in stark detail, were the familiar outlines of tiny Ceres: the bare expanse that was Ceresta's sprawling port...the geometric patterns of the town.

And there, too, in the upper scanner, shone clusters of tiny, crawling pinpoints—the mighty Federation fleet hurtling through the void, poising in this moment to lance down upon their distant prey.

IT dragged through a thousand years, that awful instant; an instant so terrible that it made the navigation room swim and dissolve before Jarl Corvett's eyes.

Why had his fate brought him here at this final moment? Why must he take his stand just in time to see the Federation fleet blast his one last dream?

Desperately, fists clenched and sweating, he tried to calculate how long it would take the racing ships to reach a range where they could use Wassreck's deadly force projectors. Five minutes—? Three?

But what did it matter? Whatever the time, it still would be too short.

Unless fate had brought him here now for a purpose; unless the gods of the void themselves were riding at his side...

His stomach writhed. With a will born of utter frenzy, he tore his eyes from the screen.

The guards and the *Fantay* officer still stood waiting. *rey* Gundre was studying him with narrowed eyes.

Cold as death, Jarl made himself stride forward. Thrusting stiff hands between the girdle and his belly, once again he spat a stream of crackling gutturals at his foes.

But then, the high commissioner was suddenly tensing, backing. "What is this?" he cried sharply. "You're no primitive!" His voice went high and raw. "Guards! Seize him—!"

The *Fantay* lunged. The guards clawed for their ray guns.

But already Jarl was pivoting, whipping a fistful of sand into the officer's eyes. He leaped back as he threw it, so that one guard was between him and the other. Savagely, he hammered home a blow; crowded close and caught the ray gun's barrel as it cleared the holster, levering it up till it tore free from the creature's tortured grasp.

Then the other guard was upon him, smashing him to his knees.

But the metal mask broke the force of the blow. Jarl triggered the ray gun. The beam lanced out, struck home at the base of the bulging jaw.

The guard fell backward.

Jarl fired again. The *Fantay* died.

But now *rey* Gundre's own weapon was out. The remaining guard came charging in.

Jarl dropped flat as the high commissioner fired. The beam passed over him; blasted the lunging guard.

Jarl shot for *rey* Gundre's weapon.

The ray gun flew out of the high commissioner's hand.

Panting, Jarl lurched to his feet. His whole body trembled. For an instant he thought he was going to faint.

Then, out of the depths of his will, new strength came. He leveled the ray gun; held it steady.

rey Gundre went white to the lips. Unsteadily, he moved backward, till his body, the palms of his hands, were pressed flat against the wall. He could not seem to tear his eyes from the hideous metal mask Jarl wore.

"Is the high commissioner afraid, then—?" Jarl laughed harshly. "Forget it, Gundre, I've things for you to do before you die."

"Jarl Corvett—!" The commissioner's eyes went wide with shock, mirror-bright with fear.

Jarl laughed again, a bleak and mirthless sound. With his free hand, he unclamped the mask; dropped it to the floor.

Tightly, he said: "Get a cross on your fleet, Commissioner. Give them their true orders—that Ceres is to be spared."

THE panic that flared in *rey* Gundre's eyes was a frightful thing to see. His face sagged, grey as lead. "No, Corvett—! Not that! I can't—!"

"Then you can die," Jarl said.

He raised the ray gun.

The high commissioner's mouth worked. "No, no…" Tottering, he stumbled towards the viziscreen.

Jarl followed him, grim as death.

The clustered pinpoints were closer to Ceres now, slashing through the void like streaks of light.

With trembling fingers, *rey* Gundre fumbled at the dials.

"Faster!" Jarl clipped. "Your life depends on it, Gundre! If they strike, you die!"

A new voice, behind them, said, "No, Jarl."

By sheer reflex, Jarl whirled.

A man stood in operation unit's doorway…a tall man with a gaunt, pain-twisted body, and high-domed head, and burning eyes:

A man Jarl Corvett knew so well—

"Wassreck—!"

"Yes, Jarl. Wassreck." The other's voice was almost gentle. The wry mouth twisted with the thin ghost of a smile.

Jarl's knees went weak as water. His gun-hand sagged. He clutched a chair to keep from falling.

Still smiling, *Ktar* Wassreck moved forward, into the navigation room. "Did I surprise you, Jarl?"

"I—thought you dead."

"And Sais, too—?" The other chuckled softly, and half-turned. "Come, my dear…"

207

And of a sudden, there was dark Sais, framed in the open doorway—radiant, lips half-parted, eyes aglow.

Ktar Wassreck said, "I know how much she means to you, my comrade. I brought her here, from Karrel's ship, to wait till you should come." His pain-warped shoulders twisted. "Because I knew you'd come, Jarl, sometime. Loyalty is a thing you understand."

"I called him on the *Knife's* screen, Jarl," Sais broke in. Her voice was warm and eager. "The crew didn't think to guard me. After that, I ran away, into the desert, and waited till the flagship came."

Jarl swayed. His brain was reeling, and everything had a queer, distorted look. He wondered if perhaps he'd finally fainted...if this were all a dream, somehow, or death.

But he made himself speak, because he had to learn the truth...find answers to the questions that kept tumbling and jumbling...

"You...were aboard the flagship—?"

"Of course, Jarl," Wassreck nodded. "I wasn't captured, nor yet did I surrender. All this has been a careful plan, worked out between the high commissioner and me."

"A—plan—?"

"Yes!" *Ktar* Wassreck's voice rang. With sudden eagerness, he leaned forward, and his eyes burned with a strange new light. "Jarl, with the power that's in these robots, the universe is ours to rule! What force is there that can stand against them? What planet could defy their might?"

"But the high commissioner..." Jarl gestured, stumbled. "Why would he aid the outlaw worlds—?" And then, in sudden panic, whirling: "Quick—! The Federation fleet—it's headed down for Ceres! We've got to stop them! It may already be too late!"

But Wassreck's voice said, "No, Jarl."

It was flat this time, no longer gentle.

SLOWLY, slowly Jarl turned from the scanner, with its clustered, crawling pinpoints. A seeping emptiness was rising in him—an ugly, hollow feeling he'd never felt before.

Wassreck still stood in the same spot as before. But now, his right hand was at waist-level.

It held a blaster.

In a voice not even remotely resembling his own, Jarl asked, "What do you mean?"

Wassreck's eyes were burning coals. His gaunt face seemed even thinner than before.

He said: "I mean the outlaw worlds must die!"

Jarl nodded slowly. "I guessed that would be it."

"Don't you see, Jarl—?" Sais cried, coming to him. "The raiders will never lose their idiot dreams of freedom! Always, everywhere, they'll make trouble! It would be madness to leave them with Ceresta and their fleet. The Federation planets know what it means to bow before a ruler—"

Wordless, Jarl looked down at her.

Hand on his arm, she rushed on—glowing, eager: "At first my father thought of you as dangerous. But always, I've loved you. That's why I came to you on Ceres, saying he was captured—so that you would prove your loyalty to him. Now, he knows; and the two of you can rule together. You and I— we'll have each other…"

She pressed against Jarl—body warm, hair soft and fragrant.

Wassreck broke in: "Jarl, you saw what happened today when I tried out that robot on Bor Legat's ships! And once the raider fleet is smashed, there'll be no opposition."

The numb emptiness filled Jarl to overflowing. "And if I say no—?"

He could see the other stiffen.

"Is there a choice?" Wassreck's laugh was suddenly savage. "Your ray-gun's down, and my blaster's on you. Even if you could kill me, the crew knows you're here; they'd be waiting for you."

And Sais whispered, "Jarl, why should you die for nothing? What can it gain you, or anyone else?" Her cool fingers caressed him. "Jarl, don't you understand? I love you! I want us to be together, now and forever…"

Jarl stood very still.

HOW many nights had he lain in a chill, lonely bunk far out in space, and dreamed of Sais beside him? How many times had he cursed the raider way, the blood and iron, and longed instead for power and booty?

Now he could have those things. What made him hang back? Why did he hesitate?

Why indeed, when refusal meant death without gain, without meaning?

Only then he thought of other things, and pain came in a rush to fill the emptiness.

For he thought of those who lived, and those who'd died, whether they lived or died for good or evil. Of Bor Legat and Ungo, Tas Karrel and Ylana, a thousand fallen crewmen.

Of Ceresta's teeming hives, and Pallas, and of the raider fleet. Of freedom.

Perhaps there was still a place in this mad universe for a man who did not fear to die.

Again, he looked down into Sais' dark, lovely face. Again, her hair's fragrance rose like perfume in his nostrils.

But as he stared, somehow, the lines and contours kept shifting, changing, till it was as if he were gazing at one of the primitives' hideous, leering masks.

Bleakly, he pushed her away. Her face sagged, incredulous.

But it was *Ktar* Wassreck himself who spoke: "You know what this means, Jarl—?"

"I know."

"Then it doesn't count that I came for you on Horla? Loyalty means nothing…?"

"Loyalty—?" Jarl laughed a bitter laugh. "And what are you loyal to, then. Wassreck? Your friends who'll die down on Ceresta?"

The gaunt man's face grew cold and bleak. He did not answer.

Jarl turned his head; slashed out at *rey* Gundre, still standing by the viziscreen: "You, Commissioner! What are you loyal to? The Federation, that you betray? Ylana, your own daughter, who'd rather die in the desert than live here with you?"

A trace of color came to the high commissioner's grey, sagging face. Unspeaking, he looked away.

"Loyalty—!" Jarl spat. "How can any of you even pretend to know what it means? Because a man's first loyalty is to his own conscience—and conscience is a thing you neither have nor understand!"

Wassreck's gaunt face contorted. "A pretty speech—to die with."

His finger went white on the blaster's trigger.

Jarl Corvett whipped up his ray gun.

YET even in that moment, Jarl knew the truth: that his strength had gone; that he was too slow. Before he could even fire himself. Wassreck would kill him.

But he didn't care to die—not while *Ktar* Wassreck still lived and held the secret of the mighty warrior robots. Too much was at stake. Too many could suffer.

Only now, there was nothing he could do. At last, the gods of the void had ridden on their way without him.

But then, incredibly, another figure hurtled across his field of vision.

The figure of High Commissioner *rey* Gundre.

For a split second. Wassreck's eyes wavered.

Jarl dived to one side as the blaster roared. The bolt seared a flaming path diagonally along his ribs.

But now, Jarl, too, was firing—lancing a ray-beam into Wassreck's midriff.

The gaunt body stiffened...straightened...fell.

Jarl threw himself round, searching for Sais—and *rey* Gundre.

They lay in a tumbled heap near the farthest wall. The commissioner was twitching, moaning faintly. Jarl stumbled across to where he lay, tried to help him to turn over.

A blaster bolt had taken the man high in the chest. Blood already was trickling from his mouth. "Ylana—! he gasped, then choked on the blood.

A moment later, he died. Jarl turned to Sais.

She, too, was dead. She held a blaster in her hand—and her neck was broken.

Dully, head throbbing, Jarl remembered *rey* Gundre's mad, unexplained rush.

Now it needed no explanation.

Outside, someone was pounding on the door. Dim sounds of tumult sifted through the portal.

So the guards had come already...

Struggling to his feet again, Jarl made his way to the viziscreen. He had lost all track of time. He half expected to find Ceres already blasted, broken.

It still was there. But the clustered pinpoints that were the Federation fleet had begun converging high above, readying for the final plunge.

With trembling fingers, Jarl set a cross for the lead ship: switched on the communicator unit. Harshly, in *rey* Gundre's name, he rasped out orders.

The wheeling ships veered; peeled off on a different course.

Ceres was saved.

Jarl sagged against the screen.

He felt incredibly old, incredibly weary.

The pounding on the door grew louder.

Jarl thought: *Another minute and they'll break in...*

And he would die.

ONLY all at once, he didn't care.

His job was done. What difference did it make, what happened now?

His only regret was that Ylana would never know that at the last, when the crisis came, her father had broken down and died to save him.

And Sais... What things had been in her mind when she raised that blaster to try to kill the man she claimed to love?

It was strange, though: he felt no hatred towards her.

But, neither did he feel love, or sorrow, or pity. It was as if she were an utter stranger, some passerby he'd never known.

So different from Ylana...

Ylana the golden. He spoke her name aloud, and liked its sound.

Ylana the golden. Red lips, grey eyes, and rippling hair.

Such queer things to be thinking about at a time like this. But then, his whole state of mind just now was somewhat queer.

Out in the hall, some heavy object smashed against the door. Soon, he knew the panel would crash down.

Why wait for it? Why not go out and meet death as a raider should?

Jarl laughed drunkenly. Reeling, he stumbled to the door; with a clumsy jerk threw back the bolt and braced himself to take the blasts.

Then the door burst open. Beings of half-a-dozen planets charged in upon him—and Big Ungo of Jupiter was in their van.

Jarl knew then that this was a nightmare—the delirium of a fevered, over-weary brain. He closed his eyes and let himself go limp; slumped to the floor.

But when he looked up again, Ungo was still there, and now Ylana, too, knelt beside him, whispering, "Jarl—! Jarl Corvett..." while the red lips quivered and tears spilled from the cool grey eyes.

Ungo said: "She made us come, Jarl—all of us that were left from Bor Legat's ships. With her to talk for us, we didn't even have to fight to get in here."

"You're lying!" Jarl accused him, twisting as pain stabbed along his wounded side. "You're not here. I'm just dreaming. When I wake up, if I'm not dead, you'll all be gone."

"No, Jarl. This isn't dreaming. This is real." All at once Ylana was smiling through her tears. "Sleep, now, Jarl. I'll still be here when you waken—or forever, if you want me…"

As she spoke, she reached out and gently closed his eyes.

He didn't mind. As a matter of fact, of a sudden he wanted to let sleep come, and quickly.

For now he knew that waking would be better than any dream.

THE END

If you've enjoyed this book, you will not want to miss these terrific titles…

If you've enjoyed this book, you will not want to miss these terrific titles…

ARMCHAIR SCI-FI & HORROR DOUBLE NOVELS, $12.95 each

D-21   **EMPIRE OF EVIL** by Robert Arnette
THE SIGN OF THE TIGER by Alan E. Nourse & J. A. Meyer

D-22   **OPERATION SQUARE PEG** by Frank Belknap Long
ENCHANTRESS OF VENUS by Leigh Brackett

D-23   **THE LIFE WATCH** by Lester Del Rey
CREATURES OF THE ABYSS by Murray Leinster

D-24   **LEGION OF LAZARUS** by Edmond Hamilton
STAR HUNTER by Andre Norton

D-25   **EMPIRE OF WOMEN** by John Fletcher
ONE OF OUR CITIES IS MISSING by Irving Cox

D-26   **THE WRONG SIDE OF PARADISE** by Raymond F. Jones
THE INVOLUNTARY IMMORTALS by Rog Phillips

D-27   **EARTH QUARTER** by Damon Knight
ENVOY TO NEW WORLDS by Keith Laumer

D-28   **SLAVES TO THE METAL HORDE** by Milton Lesser
HUNTERS OUT OF TIME by Joseph E. Kelleam

D-29   **RX JUPITER SAVE US** by Ward Moore
BEWARE THE USURPERS by Geoff St. Reynard

D-30   **SECRET OF THE SERPENT** by Don Wilcox
CRUSADE ACROSS THE VOID by Dwight V. Swain

ARMCHAIR SCIENCE FICTION CLASSICS, $12.95 each

C-7   **THE SHAVER MYSTERY, pt. 1**
by Richard S. Shaver

C-8   **THE SHAVER MYSTERY, pt. 2**
by Richard S. Shaver

C-9   **MURDER IN SPACE** by David V. Reed
by David V. Reed

ARMCHAIR MASTERS OF SCIENCE FICTION SERIES, $16.95 each

M-3   **MASTERS OF SCIENCE FICTION, Vol. Three**
Robert Sheckley, "The Perfect Woman" and other tales

M-4   **MASTERS OF SCIENCE FICTION, Vol. Four**
Mack Reynolds, "Stowaway" and other tales